CW01271233

DARK EDGE PRESS

FAMILY FIRST

TONY MILLINGTON

Published in 2021 by Dark Edge Press

Y Bwthyn
Caerleon Road,
Newport,
Wales.

www.darkedgepress.co.uk

Text copyright © 2021 Tony Millington

Cover Design: Jamie Curtis

Cover Photography: © Canva

A CIP catalogue record for this book is available from the British Library.

ISBN (eBook): 978-1-5272-9022-8
ISBN (Paperback): 979-8-7717-8054-2

To my rocks: my wife Ann, and my son Richard.

CONTENTS

CHAPTER ONE

TUESDAY, 11.30 p.m.

Ronald Freeman downed the dregs of his final pint and said goodnight to the landlord of his local pub, The Dragon's Den.

He'd been cheering on their pool team, who had beaten The King's Head 7-2 in the local league. The last to leave, having consumed far too much alcohol, he staggered through the back door of the pub towards the car park. He zig-zagged across the potholes in the tarmac, trying to avoid tripping over them, towards his car. It had been raining most of the evening, leaving the holes full of water.

He lit his last cigarette and threw away the empty packet. As he reached the car door, he fumbled for the keys in his trouser pocket, dropping them on the ground, and muttering under his breath. Leaning over, he grabbed them before opening the door of the battered silver VW Passat, parked haphazardly next to a wall at the back of the car park.

Freeman slid into the driver's seat and started the engine, doing the seatbelt up, with the cigarette hanging from his mouth. There was a sharp knock on the driver's window. Puzzled, he wound the window down and glared through the cigarette smoke and beer haze to see a human form standing by his car.

'Mr Ronald Freeman?' the stranger asked.

'Yes? And who the fuck wants to know?' Freeman snarled back.

'This is for Fredrick Mason,' Colin Littlewood calmly said. With that, he fired twice into the car. The back of Freeman's head exploded as the bullets entered his forehead, showering the inside of the car with pieces of skull and brain matter. He slumped in the seat, held in place only by his seatbelt.

Littlewood stuffed his gun into the deep pocket of his donkey jacket and disappeared into the shadows.

-X-

Colin Littlewood knew where Freeman would be that night. Having watched him for over a week, Littlewood had followed Freeman at a safe distance whilst working out the best time and place to kill him. He discovered the security lights were not powerful enough to reach the back corners of the car park, an excellent place to wait in the shadows near the industrial-sized bins. It was the ideal place to put a bullet in Freeman's head without being noticed. Unfortunately, as he waited he had to endure the terrible smell of the pub waste in the bins, but the result was worth it. Though he wished he had chosen a different coat to wear. The donkey jacket was heavy after the latest torrential downpour.

Most of Freeman's visits to the Dragon's Den ended up with him leaving completely hammered. How he could drive in that state, without getting pulled over or crashing, was a mystery to Littlewood. He had watched Freeman say good night to the landlord as he was locking up. Freeman had then staggered all the way to the car, trying to light a cigarette. When he had managed to open the car and get inside, Littlewood had made his move.

2

He'd enjoyed putting two bullets in that scumbags head. He walked through the back gate at the far end of the car park and into the darkness, checked around to ensure that nobody had seen a thing and, feeling euphoric said to himself, 'One down.'

He smiled. Revenge was sweet.

-X-

Terry Watson was turning off the lights and getting into bed, when the *War of the Worlds* theme music blared from his phone.

His wife Sally scowled; first at the clock which read midnight and then back at him. 'Who could be ringing at this time of night?' she asked sarcastically, sighing because she already knew the answer.

Terry thought about cracking a joke but decided now was not the best time. He picked up the phone from the bedside table. 'Watson?'

'I'll be outside in five,' Keith Monteith announced as he flung himself into the driver's seat of his two-year-old blue BMW 1 series. Monteith was Watson's partner-in-crime, or crime prevention, as they occasionally joked.

'Where's the fire?'

'No fire. It's a shooting,' Monteith responded, as he started the engine.

'I'll be waiting.' Watson heard the car wheels spin as Monteith pulled away before disconnecting from the hands-free.

Watson quickly threw on a pair of jeans, socks and a clean shirt, as Sally looked on. He checked he had everything including his police ID, warrant card, and radio.

'Do you have to go?' Sally said nervously as she got out of bed, wearing just a white T-shirt with Bugs Bunny on it. She hated when he had to rush off to a call where a serious crime had been committed. She dreaded to think the kind of risk he was going to face. What if one day she got the call, or the visit, that every wife feared? To say that he wouldn't be coming home. She followed him out of the bedroom as he pulled on his leather jacket.

'After fifteen years of marriage you still ask me that.' Watson turned when he reached the top of the stairs and kissed her.

'Yes, because I care, you silly sod.' Sally sighed loudly, taking one last cuddle before he walked down the stairs.

'Love you,' he called as he opened the front door.

'Love you too, darling.' She watched him disappear and heard him lock the door behind him.

'Where's Daddy going?' a tired voice called out from her bedroom.

Sally opened the door. Their six-year-old daughter Rachel was sitting up in bed. 'He has to go into work little miss, and you should be asleep. Did we wake you?' Sally entered the room and tucked her back in.

'I heard Dad's phone going off and both of you talking,' Rachel said as she lay back down and rubbed her closing eyes.

'He will be back soon darling. Now I think we should both try to get some sleep.' She kissed her daughter on the forehead. 'Goodnight sweetie.'

The little girl, half asleep, cuddled up to her favourite teddy bear dressed as a policeman. 'Night, Mum.'

As Watson shut and locked the front door, Monteith was already outside waiting. His car's headlights showed a fine rain was still falling. Watson jumped into the passenger seat.

'Got out alive then?' Monteith said, as he floored the BMW.

'Yes. Sally was fine. Wasn't Katie?'

'I think the last thing I heard her mumble beneath the duvet was piss off and save the world then,' Monteith laughed.

CHAPTER TWO

Detective Sergeants Monteith and Watson had been partners in the Criminal Detective Agency of the West Ravenswood Police Force for the last five years.

West Ravenswood was a small city with a population of around 150,000. It was much like every other UK city or town. It had areas you would love to live, but can't afford, areas you wouldn't live even if someone paid you to, and some that were okay, the middle of the road areas.

The detectives had gone to school together, graduated in the same year, and then qualified for the Police Training Centre at Hendon. After their initial two year PC training and neighbourhood/response training, they were posted to different areas of policing. When the force set up the CDA, both had made detective grade and were the obvious candidates to be assigned to it, beating a strong short-list.

They were even each other's best man at their weddings.

Reaching the crime scene, Monteith parked up on the street in front of The Dragon's Den in the Bankside part of the city. They had secured the area with crime tape, across the gateway at the side of the pub.

Floodlights illuminated the car park at the rear, reaching into the areas the security light could not. A tent was erected to cover the car from onlookers and prevent any potential evidence contamination. Under the tent, the forensic investigators were carefully going over the VW Passat with its driver's door open.

As they walked past, Watson and Monteith could see the body in the car through the flap in the tent. It was not a pretty sight.

Sergeant Karl Lorimer acting as Trainee Detective Sergeant greeted them and led them into the pub via the back door, along a corridor and past the toilets to where the bar was situated, splitting the lounge with its cosy snug, soft furnishings and low lighting – the door to the restaurant and kitchen at the far end of the room – from a games area. It wasn't quite spit and sawdust, but not far off. There were large, dirty, cream-coloured tiles on the floor. The walls and ceiling were stained dirty nicotine yellow, remnants from when smoking was still allowed inside. On the walls were the obligatory two pictures of dressed-up dogs playing pool and cards. Two large windows looked out onto the street. Blue baize coloured pool table at the far end on the room, along with a dart board. A Wurlitzer jukebox stood next to the corridor which led out to the toilets and back door. The lighting came from three shaded lights in the ceiling and two wall lights.

The landlord, Mr Preston sat at the bar, nursing a whisky.

'He's given us the victim's name,' TDS Lorimer said in a hushed tone, 'but nothing else.'

Watson went over to the landlord, introduced himself, and sat down on a barstool.

'What can you tell us, Mr Preston?'

'I'd just shown Ronald to the door and said good night. I locked up and then a couple of minutes later I heard two bangs.'

Preston paused and gulped down the whole of the large whisky in one.

'I thought he was having trouble with his car, backfiring. I can't remember how many times I said he should get a better one. I unlocked and went out of the door, and saw . . .'

With that he collapsed in tears, his body and shoulders heaving up and down as the shock of the night hit him. Watson leaned over and placed a hand on his shoulder and quietly thanked him, before getting up and strolling over to where Monteith and the sergeant were standing near the jukebox.

'We won't get much out of him tonight,' Watson said looking back at Preston. 'Let's see what we can find outside.'

Back out in the car park, the rain had thankfully stopped. Both tried to do a quick step around the water-filled pot holes. Watson failed and his right foot went straight into one. 'Bollocks!' he said, shaking his foot to get most of the water off.

'Good job there were floodlights on or you would have got both feet wet!' Monteith laughed. Watson just shook his head.

The Home Office pathologist James Macintosh, or Mac the Knife as they called him, had arrived and was under the tent studying Ronald Freeman's body.

'Hi Mac, what we got?' Monteith said.

'A bloody mess that's what. Why can't killers just put the bullets into the body instead of having to blow a person's brains half out! Would make my job a lot easier. Now I will have to pick this car apart to get the rest of this head.'

'But you love it, don't you Mac?' Monteith grinned, trying to make light of the situation.

'Yes, great fun trying to do a skull jigsaw, then

finding out there is a piece missing.'

'The landlord said he heard two bangs,' Watson interjected.

'Yes . . . that would cause this mess. Not sure about the calibre until we find the bullets. Will let you know when I get him back to the lab.'

'Have you found any identification?'

'There's a wallet here with a driving licence belonging to Ronald Freeman.' Mac handed it over in a clear evidence bag to Watson.

'That name ties in with what the landlord said. Okay Mac, it seems that you have everything under control here. See you back at the station.' With that they left Mac and his team to their job.

CHAPTER THREE

Littlewood parked his car on the drive next to his daughter's.

Opening the front door of his terrace house, with one final glance around at the street to make sure nobody had seen him, he entered and locked it behind him. He put his wet donkey jacket on the hanger behind the door. Satisfied with his night's work he walked into the front room. His daughter Susan was sitting on the sofa with her legs tucked up under her watching a film on Netflix. She glanced round as he entered.

'Enjoyed your evening?' she said.

'Yes, very enjoyable,' he replied, leaning over and kissing her forehead. He watched the film she had on for a couple of minutes. *One Flew Over the Cuckoo's Nest.* He had seen it more times than he cared to remember.

'I think I'll go up. See you in the morning, sweetheart.'

Susan turned her head towards him, 'Night, Dad.'

Littlewood removed the gun from his coat and took it upstairs to his bedroom. Opening the wardrobe knelt down and pulled out an old rucksack which he had tucked away at the back. He put the gun deep inside the rucksack and removed a red bound book. Opening it, and using the pen attached, he put a line through the first name on the list, Ronald Freeman.

-X-

Detective Chief Inspector Kenneth Crompton had been the head of the CDA since its conception five years ago, with over twenty years of policing behind him.

The agency was on the fourth floor of the main Police Headquarters in the city centre. Crompton was big in stature, both in build and reputation. He had risen through the ranks as a career policeman and now was the head of the newest part of the area's force. Always called a spade a spade and did not like people bullshitting him, but there to help anyone who needed it.

At 1 a.m., he was still sat behind his large wooden desk in his glass-walled office. When Watson and Monteith arrived back, he waved them in as he finished speaking on the phone.

'The press office is looking for a heads up, so what have we got?' Crompton said as Watson and Monteith sat in the leather-backed chairs on the other side of his desk.

Watson began. 'We've just got back from the shooting at The Dragon's Den. White male shot whilst sitting in his car in the pub's car park around 11.30 p.m. last night. The landlord said after locking up he heard two loud bangs. He ran out into the car park at the back of the pub and found the man's body in his car.'

'Did he know who the victim was?'

'The name he has given is the same as on the victim's driving licence. Ronald Freeman.'

Crompton sat bolt upright. 'What? Who?'

'The victim is Ronald Freeman,' Watson repeated. They both watched as the colour drained from their DCI's face. 'Are you all right, Sir?' Monteith pitched in, 'You look like you've seen a ghost!'

Crompton rose out of his chair and went to his cabinet, opened the bottom drawer and pulled out a bottle of whisky. He poured two shots and sat back down, his face ashen.

'Ronald Freeman is a blast from the past. One of my first cases as a detective.' Crompton took a swig of his whisky.

'He was jailed for the manslaughter of a shop owner, Fred Mason, fifteen years ago. Everyone working the case said it should have been murder. He went into the place to rob it with a sawn off shotgun. Mason did not give in and tackled him. The gun went off in the struggle. Mason died of his wounds a few days later.'

Crompton paused, looking like he was thinking back to that dreaded day. He gave a big sigh. His voice was barely above a whisper.

'Until you said his name I didn't know they had released him, never mind he was back in the city.'

Crompton looked shaken as if a ghost had walked over his grave. He finished his drink, his hand tightly gripping the glass.

'Boss, are you ok?' Monteith said.

'Yes, yes. Go home and get some rest, lads. We will continue this when you come back.'

'You're sure?' Watson said.

'Yes, go on. I've still got things to do.'

As they left, Crompton, deep in thought, stood by the window looking down on the bright lights of the city centre. Only one question was on his mind. Why?

CHAPTER FOUR

WEDNESDAY MORNING

Monteith and Watson had gone back home for a few hours' sleep around 2 a.m.

They returned to the office for the 9.30 a.m. debrief following. Pathologist James Macintosh was there to present his initial findings and DCI Crompton held court in his office. Strong coffee and bacon rolls from the cafe down the street were the order of the morning, seeing as each of them had had less than five hours' sleep.

Crompton, who had not been home and was still in his clothes from yesterday, started.

'Okay folks, last night's shooting. Mac, your findings, please.'

'I've not done a full post-mortem yet, but it's safe to say Ronald Freeman was shot twice at point blank range, in through the forehead and out of the back of the head. The two holes in the forehead suggest that the killer was outside the car and fired down through the driver's window. What's left of the bullets recovered from the car suggests they were 9mm. Forensics were still there completing their search of the car and the car park when I left around 2 a.m.'

'Thanks Mac,' Crompton said, wiping his mouth with a paper napkin after finishing his bacon roll.

'We need to find out whether who shot him was in the pub with Freeman, waited until he left, or if the killer was already waiting outside for him. Watson and Monteith can you go back and see if the landlord is up to answering any more questions, please? We need to know who visited the pub last night. Did anybody confront Freeman whilst he was in there? Did he piss anyone off during the evening? I'll get uniform to carry out door-to-door enquiries in the area this morning.'

Monteith put his coffee down on the desk. 'Boss, before we go, you said last night you knew Freeman and remembered why he got put away. Can you enlighten us?'

Crompton leaned back in his chair and gathered himself together, struggling with his thoughts. 'I had been promoted to detective about two months earlier, and this was my first big case. Freeman entered Fred Mason's Newsagents in the evening with a shotgun to rob it. He brandished the gun at the young girl behind the counter, Mason's daughter, and demanded the money from the till. Fred Mason was stacking shelves in the shop, and when he heard Freeman he came out and confronted him. Mason made a lunge for the gun to protect his daughter. During the struggle the gun went off. Mason suffered serious wounds to his chest and died in hospital two days later. Freeman ran out of the shop taking nothing. Up until that evening he had only been a petty criminal, although he had been in prison before. Mason's daughter identified Freeman from mug shots.'

Crompton slurped down his coffee. 'We were confident he would get put away for murder, but to our horror his defence barrister was so good the jury only convicted him of manslaughter. He got sixteen years in Claythorn Prison. That was twelve years ago. That's why I was stunned he was out.'

The room fell silent as they took it in. Monteith nudged Watson and caught Mac's eye. He signalled to the door to leave Crompton with his thoughts.

Monteith turned back and in a low voice said, 'Boss, don't worry, we will catch the person who did this.' Crompton looked up and nodded.

Watson and Monteith got back into the BMW, which was parked round the back of the headquarters, and headed back to the Dragon's Den.

'Have you noticed that he is still shook up over this Freeman shooting?' Watson commented.

'I bet it's nothing. It's because as he said, Freeman was his first case.' Monteith said. 'We all remember our first cases. It was part of the thrill back then. Now they all seem to roll into one another. Ours was that drug bust at that cannabis factory. I remember still being high on the fumes the plants gave off the next day. The clearance team had to do it in twenty minute shifts because there were many plants and the smell they gave off affected them so much.'

'Yes I remember, but I don't know, I think there's something more to this,' Watson sounded unsure.

'You're reading too much into it Terry, lighten up.' With that Monteith flattened the accelerator and shot down the high street.

'Slow down, you idiot. I don't want to end up on Mac's table just yet,' Watson shouted grabbing onto the sides of his seat.

CHAPTER FIVE

Back at the Dragon's Den, they found the press assembled behind the tape which had been strung up across the end of the road.

This would be a pain for the morning travellers as the pub was on a bus route. Once they were let through, Monteith had to park his car on the road as crime scene tape was still across the gate leading to the car park. They showed their badges to the Police Constable on the gate guarding the scene, and ducked under the tape. As they walked around the side of the pub into the car park, the forensic technicians were packing their gear away into a white-panelled van.

'They look like beings from another planet when they're in their paper hazmat suits,' Watson commented, nudging Monteith.

'You've been watching too many sci-fi programs,' Monteith said.

'I'm glad someone has something to laugh about,' a woman shouted at them. She was standing by the pub's back door, smoking. She was small and stout and dressed in a knee-length black skirt, patterned blouse and thin cardigan.

'I'm sorry madam, it's just an internal joke. My

name is Detective Sergeant Monteith, and this is Detective Sergeant Watson.'

'I know who you are, I saw you last night. I'm Elizabeth Preston, follow me.' She put her cigarette out and led them through the door, taking them into the main area of the pub.

The cleaners were going about their business as the three of them sat at a table in the lounge area.

'Is your husband around Mrs Preston? We would like to ask him a few more questions about what happened last night,' Watson said.

'I'm sorry, he is asleep. After you left, the doctor came and gave him a sedative to calm him down and allow him some rest. Any questions you have I can help you with,' Elizabeth said resolutely.

Watson glanced at Monteith as if to say that's us told, before asking, 'Where were you last night when Ronald Freeman was killed?'

'Murdered detective, don't you forget that,' Elizabeth spat. 'I was upstairs. I'd put our two children to bed an hour before and stayed up there, until . . . you know what. I heard two loud bangs and went to look out of the window overlooking the car park. Peter, my husband, came running out from the back door. He went across to Ronald's car and looked through the window, threw up by the wall, then shouted up at me to call the police. Which I did.'

'Did you see anybody else in the car park?'

'No,' Elizabeth paused, 'I didn't think about it until now, but I thought I saw the gate at the far end of the car park swing shut before Peter came out.'

'Where does that gate lead to?' Watson said, jotting everything down.

'There is a large pathway which runs behind us and the other terrace houses on this side of the street. The refuse lorries and some delivery vans use it.'

'Can you remember when you went upstairs who was down here in the bar, Mrs Preston?'

'Only Peter, Ronald and two other regulars who only live across the street – so they would have gone out the front door. We'd had a pool match earlier in the evening, but they'd all left by the time Peter locked up.'

A cleaner came into the lounge and started to polish the tables.

'Can you hang on, June, till we've finished?' Elizabeth said, trying to keep calm.

'Oh, sorry,' the cleaner replied, as she picked up her bucket and went back out.

'Was Ronald a regular?' Monteith continued.

'Yes, three or four times a week he comes in.' She paused. 'Came in.'

'Always the same days each week?' Watson said.

'Yes, when the pool or darts teams are playing at home. He didn't play, but he liked to cheer them on.'

Watson and Monteith glanced again at each other. Elizabeth noticed and sat up straight.

'Do you think someone planned this?' Her eyes wide open with fright. Her mind going into overdrive with what the detectives were thinking.

'Well, we don't know yet, we have only just started the investigation. Did anyone cause him any trouble in here last night?' Watson tried to recover the situation.

'No,' Elizabeth said forcefully. 'Now leave and get out and catch the bastard who killed him'. With that she got up and turned away from them, standing staring through the front window, arms folded, a look of despair on her face. Tears welling up.

Watson and Monteith got up and made their way to the door.

Monteith stopped and said, 'One last question, Mrs Preston. The address on his driving licence is on the other side of town. Why did he make this pub his local?'

Elizabeth turned back to them wearing a confused look on her face. 'Don't you know? Ronald Freeman was my brother.'

CHAPTER SIX

WEDNESDAY AFTERNOON

Littlewood was back on the move. He wanted to check on the next person on his list, Jackson Davis.

Of all the people he had marked down, this one made his skin crawl and his blood boil. Jackson had tortured and killed two sex workers twenty-five years ago. Even though he had served his time and was in his early sixties, Littlewood was not prepared to let this murderer go unpunished. He had been watching Davis for about a week now, working out his routines.

Today, as always, Jackson took his Alsatian for a walk in the park across the road from his house. Littlewood parked his red Škoda Fabia on a nearby street, locked it up and went into the park.

He wandered around for a couple of minutes, taking in the afternoon sun before sitting on a bench, not too close to Davis, but close enough to watch him. He picked up a newspaper which had been left, giving the impression he was reading to anyone passing by. The park was not one of the biggest in the city. It had big green spaces with pathways criss-crossing; flower beds were in full bloom, with trees lining the pathways around the edge. Mothers with small children were making the most of the weather, getting out of the house with their kids for some fresh air before they went crazy.

Davis was there talking to the youngsters using the gym equipment, teaching them the best way of doing dips and pull-ups on the bars. Davis may have been 62, but he still carried a big physical presence. Littlewood could visualise him trying to keep fit in the prison's gym. He thought prisons shouldn't have things like that.

Prison was a punishment and shouldn't be a holiday camp, was Littlewood's belief. He had read in some online newspaper article that most prisons provided satellite television and computer games for their guests at Her Majesty's pleasure. One, they said, had a state of the art well-equipped gym. It angered him. More than £20 a month for Mr law-abiding Joe Bloggs on the outside, free for the scum on the inside. A complete waste of tax payers' money.

After about thirty minutes of watching and reviewing his surroundings, Littlewood had seen all he needed. This takeout would be a lot harder than Freeman. More in-depth planning was needed, and the park was not the place to do it. He would have loved to walk over to Davis and pull the trigger on him there and then, but that was not how he planned to do it. He wanted to savour Davis's demise, put him through the same horrors the sex workers suffered.

Returning to his car, he made notes in his red book, and left to plan Davis's death.

Jackson Davis had clocked the loner on the bench.

A single man on his own, looking so far out of place in a park full of mothers and children, dog walkers and teenagers. All he needed was a sign around his neck saying 'loser.'

Davis couldn't care less who he was, a father trying to get a glimpse of his children after a divorce, the police doing undercover surveillance on somebody. Maybe him for all he knew. A looney fan trying to get close to him.

They existed. There were other jailbirds he was in with who received so-called fan mail, from the public. Pen pals they called it. He couldn't work out who had fewer morals, the ones in jail or the ones that sent the letters.

Davis let the loner leave first, and then he said his goodbyes to the teenagers at the gym equipment. As he was going out of the gate, he put his dog's poo in the doggie bin. He crossed the road with his Alsatian by his side and went up the gravel drive past his black Toyota RAV4, to his house.

He let his dog off the lead once they got inside. The dog's tail wagged hard, his nose to the floor until he got to his water bowl for a long drink. Davis made his way up the carpeted stairs to his bedroom, opened the glass-fronted wardrobe and flicked through his stylish shirts. He smiled to himself as he picked out his outfit for the evening's entertainment. Tonight he would go out on the town and have fun. His kind of fun.

-X-

They were all gathered around the large whiteboard attached to the wall which held all the information they'd gathered so far. It wasn't much, other than the pictures of Ronald Freeman's body, slumped in the car. Gruesome that it was. Pictures of some things the forensics team found in the car park and pictures of what was left of the bullets.

'What else do we have?' Crompton said frustratingly, as he sat on the edge of a desk in the main office.

'The door-to-door came up with nothing. Nobody was around that time of night,' Lorimer said, sitting at his desk looking at his notes. 'One or two said they heard something but upon looking out of their windows, they saw nothing. The alleyway at the back of the houses is very dimly lit.'

Crompton nodded and turned to Watson. 'Did you get anything from Mr Preston?'

'We didn't see Mr Preston,' Watson started. 'But we spoke to his wife Elizabeth. She said she was Ronald's sister.' Watson watched his boss carefully in case there was any change in his face. Nothing.

'And?' Crompton pressed. He got off the desk and paced around waiting for answers.

'And she said Ronald came in three or four times a week. No problems with other customers. Nobody came in and caused him trouble. She may have seen the back gate open and close, but she cannot be certain. There could be hundreds of fingerprints on there.'

'So we have nothing from the crime scene, right?' a frustrated Crompton threw back at them. Everyone in the room went quiet and looked down to avoid his eye. Crompton stopped pacing and shouted, 'Right you lot, let's check on who his cellmates were in Claythorn. Are any of them out yet, has he kept in contact with anybody? Check his address – where is it?'

'His driving licence gave an address in Thelwell.' Monteith spoke up after Crompton's onslaught.

'Right you two, see what you find. Let's go to it.' With that, Crompton stormed back to his office and slammed the door shut. The door shook as the rest of the room exchanged glances.

Lorimer slowly shook his head. 'Is he always like that?'

'Only on his good days.' Monteith laughed.

'Remind me not to be around on his bad days. I'll need my riot gear if I am.'

Watson and Monteith went back to their desks.

'What the hell are you playing at?' Monteith hissed. 'I saw you look straight at the boss when you talked about Freeman's sister.'

'There is something the boss is not telling us, I'm sure.'

'You're nuts if you think that. You really believe he's holding something back?' Monteith pointed his finger towards Watson.

'Yes I do, but I don't know what yet.'

Monteith grabbed his car keys and made for the door. 'Come on, I don't want to spend a minute longer than I need to in Thelwell. Not in my car.'

-X-

It's safe to say that Thelwell wasn't the best part of West Ravenswood. In fact, it was considered locally as one of the worst. It was the biggest of the original council estates built when the city undertook redevelopment in the sixties. One of the ingenious Van Goghs with his spray paint had changed a street sign from, 'Welcome to Thelwell' into 'Welcome to Thelwell HELL.'

This was where most of the city's illegal activity took place. You wanted drugs, you got them here, if you were looking for stolen property, chances are you would find it here. Stolen cars were usually dumped here, either burnt out after the joy riders had finished with them, or were being welded to another car to make a cut and shut.

The address they had for Freeman turned out to be a hostel on the edge of Thelwell. Monteith was glad it wasn't in the centre of hell, but still worried about his pride and joy as he pulled into the small car park at the front. A low wall, which had seen better days, ran along the length of the car park.

They slowly got out, looking around carefully, spotting the local look outs for the gangs and ruling families in the area: kids, who had congregated on the street corner in front of a small newsagent.

'Let's make this quick. I don't want to come out and

find my tyres slashed, or a key scraped down my paintwork,' Monteith said adamantly.

'Tenner to look after your car, mister.' One kid shouted from across the road. 'I'll do it for a fiver,' another one chipped in then burst out laughing.

Monteith glanced back over his shoulder as they went up to the front door. The hostel was a three-storey building dating back to when Thelwell was first built. It started out as fancy flats but over the years owners moved out and squatters moved in. Now refurbished by the council, it had an electronic buzzer system. Watson pushed the button marked 'office.' There was a CCTV camera on the wall above the door. They waited about twenty seconds before a female voice answered.

'Yes, who is it?'

'Detective Sergeants Watson and Monteith, from the Criminal Detective Agency of the West Ravenswood Police Department madam.'

'Show your IDs to the CCTV please.'

They both took out their IDs and held them up. The door buzzed and unlocked, and they stepped through into a large hall.

'Hello, I'm Sheila Evans, the manager.' She was a tall thin lady, dressed in dungarees, yellow T-shirt and a bandana. They shook hands and Sheila directed them into her small office. She sat behind her desk, covered in paperwork and a computer. Watson looked around before sitting in one of the two guest chairs. The room was a tight squeeze, comprising the large desk, Sheila's chair, the two guest chairs, and two tall filing cabinets.

'What can I help you with, detectives?' Sheila said.

'Ronald Freeman. His driving licence gave this as his address?' Monteith started.

'Yes, he's been living here for about three months. It's very shocking, his death,' Sheila said with a quiver in her voice. 'His sister rang this morning. Do you know who it was?'

'No, it's too early in the investigation to say anything. That's why we're here. What did you say? His sister Elizabeth rang this morning?'

'Yes, she is a regular visitor here, or should I say was. Visited Ronald about three times a week. Making sure he was okay for food and other things. He moved in here just after he came out of prison. His sister arranged the accommodation for him. Tried to get him back into mainstream life. She helped him to look for a job, and to claim the benefits he was entitled to. She paid his rent as well. He spends, sorry spent, some evenings at her pub. Elizabeth mentioned him moving into a flat nearer to where she lived.'

Sheila stared out of the window at the kids outside and then back at the detectives. 'You can't blame her for wanting him to live nearer to her. You know what this area is like.'

'Did he have any other visitors besides his sister?' Monteith said.

'No . . . not that I know of. But I heard him say a couple of times over the last week or so that he thought he was being followed. Elizabeth put it down to paranoia. Being cooped up in prison all that time watching your back and then released into society. I suppose you are bound to feel . . . well vulnerable, shall we say.'

'Did he give you or his sister a description of the person he thought might be following him?'

'No, but, as I said before, you know what this area is like. Kids and other people hanging around the streets, looking after number one, or who pays them as look outs. He might have mistaken one of them. If there was a stranger around this area, then word soon gets out. The local grapevine stretches a long way and is quick.'

'Any chance we can we look in his room?' Watson said.

'I'm afraid I cannot allow that. Not unless you have a warrant and his sister is present. She has asked for nobody to go in for now.'

There was a knock on the office door. 'Yes?' Sheila said.

A young man stuck his head round the door. 'Sorry didn't know you had company. Sheila, one of the bulbs has blown on the second floor landing.'

'Okay, Mike, I will be there soon, thank you. Detectives, I'm sorry to cut this short but looks like I am wanted. No rest for the workers. I will see you out.'

There were still kids and teenagers hanging around across the street by the shop. Monteith quickly went over to his car to check it still had four wheels, and the paint was intact.

'Do you get a lot of trouble with the kids round here?' Watson said to Sheila, as Monteith was frantically looking for his keys.

'Funnily enough, no. They know what happens in this area stays in this area, and you do nothing to your neighbour. They look after their own here, including us. Hope you catch the bastard that did this.' With that Sheila disappeared inside.

CHAPTER SEVEN

Monteith dropped Watson back at his house. They were both tired and pissed off due to a four car pile-up on the dual carriageway which had added over an hour onto their usual thirty-minute journey.

It was a large four bedroom detached, in the South Meadows area of the city. Watson walked up his gravel driveway past his blue Ford Focus and his wife Sally's red Citroen Picasso. The Picasso was on its last legs but they needed to keep it going for now. He noticed the front lawn needed cutting, and the borders needed weeding and tidying up too. A job for the weekend he thought, already feeling exhausted at the prospect of gardening on his day off.

What Watson needed right now was a hot shower, something to eat and hopefully, a massage from Sally. He opened the front door to a wall of noise. How four people can make that much noise he would never work out, he thought as he closed the door behind him. Rachel was in her pink elephant pyjamas in the lounge, singing along loudly to her music.

The two eldest children, Simon, thirteen, and eleven-year-old Jason were arguing upstairs about something to do with a console game. Sally stood at the bottom of the stairs with her back to him, trying to regain order. Watson took in her lovely figure, dressed in a tight red T-shirt, and a well-fitting pair of worn jeans. He smiled at the thought of that massage later and hoped Sally wouldn't be too tired.

The stairs doubled back on themselves. Coming off the hall was the lounge which ran the full length of the house, walls covered in family photographs and signed framed posters of his favourite rock bands. The hall continued through to a large kitchen with all mod cons and red shiny cabinets. Off the kitchen was a toilet and wet room.

'Here's the cavalry,' Sally said turning, smiling at Terry.

'Nope, only The Lone Ranger, Tonto has just left.' He pulled Sally into an embrace and kissed her gently on the lips.

'Daddy!' Rachel squealed as she spotted him and charged across the lounge and out into the hall. Terry bent down and picked her up, swinging her around, with her long hair flying behind her. Her laughter filled the house.

'I'm listening to my music, here listen.' With that she put her earphones on his head. Terry hadn't got the foggiest what he was listening to, but bobbed his head along with it, trying to sing along with the words, making Rachel giggle and Sally shake her head in amusement. Rachel took the headphones back off his head.

'I was enjoying that,' he said faking upset but with a big smile on his face.

'You're funny Daddy,' Rachel said still giggling.

'Right young lady, I said you could stay up until Daddy came in,' Sally broke the revelry.

'Aww, he only just got in!' Rachel said with a pout.

'Go on up angel. I'll come and say goodnight once you're ready for bed,' said Terry, herding her toward the stairs and clapping his hands, chuckling at her expression as she stomped upstairs.

'Food or shower first, Mr Lone Ranger?' Sally said as she was wrapped up from behind in Terry's arms.

'Food first, I might need help in the shower later!'
'Oh, really?' Sally turned around with an impish grin on her face.

CHAPTER EIGHT

On the other side of the city, Jackson Davis stopped his black Toyota in Austin Lane, part of the red light district.

Winding down the passenger window, he beckoned a small redhead over who was standing on her own next to a high wall. She was only five feet, six inches in her red shiny high heels, if that, and wore a small red sequined crop top and a black leather look mini skirt which left nothing to the imagination.

'Fancy a good night?' she said through the window, while playing with her hair teasingly.

Davis smiled, patting the passenger seat, 'Get in and I will give you the best night of your life.'

But before she could open the door, Littlewood ran out of the dim light, shoved her out of the way, and piled into the back seat of Davis's car. He pulled out his Glock and pointed it at Davis.

'Drive now if you know what's good for you,' Littlewood bellowed.

Davis was stunned, wildly thinking about what he could do.

'Drive!' Littlewood repeated, hitting the back of the driver's seat to add emphasis to his words.

Davis shoved his car in gear, and wheel spun it

away from the kerb, leaving the small redhead sprawled out on the pavement instead of where she should be, in his car.

'Drive where?' he said, feeling the lump in his throat, and glancing in the rear-view mirror to try to glimpse this mad stranger in the back of his car by using the passing street lights.

'The Barton Industrial Estate. And if you see a police car or try to signal to anyone, I will shoot you right here and now.' Littlewood acted in a calm and measured manner, settling back but still with his Glock trained onto Davis.

'What do you want? Money? My car? You can have it all. All you have to do is say, I'll pull over and you can take it.' Davis was trying to work out who his unwanted passenger was. They moved out of the outer city centre on the main dual carriageway, and towards the Marsh Mills Trading Estate which housed Barton Industrial Estate.

Littlewood spoke in an authoritative voice. 'Jackson Davis, former gym instructor. Jailed for torturing and killing two sex workers twenty-five years ago. Released on licence. What would the authorities think if they knew you were bothering sex workers again? Naughty, naughty.'

How does he know all this?

David took his time to reply. 'You have me at a disadvantage. You know all about me but I don't know you.'

'Just shut up and drive,' Littlewood's responded, unaware that things were about to change.

As they came off the dual carriageway and entered the trading estate, they passed through a section of a well-lit road. Davis looked in the rear-view mirror, realising who his passenger was. A smile passed across his face, ending in a huge grin and a little laugh.

'What are you laughing at?' Littlewood said, sitting forward a little with his hand gripping his gun tighter.

'Did you have a good time in the park today?'

'What are you on about?' Littlewood tried to remain calm, but he felt flustered.

'Oh, come on Colin. That is your name isn't it? Colin Littlewood? You were in the park earlier on, watching me. You thought I hadn't noticed you?' Davis relaxed a little. Was enjoying himself, even. 'Or should I say former prison officer Colin Littlewood? Medically retired through stress and a breakdown following the murder of your wife Jackie. I believe you were on the night shift at Claythorn Prison. Two kids broke into your house, if I remember. Your wife disturbed them and . . . well . . .' Davis trailed off with a sly smile.

'How the fuck do you know that?' It was Littlewood's turn to be surprised. He had a sinking feeling that everything was unravelling quickly.

'I was in Claythorn when it happened, surely you haven't forgotten that? It was all over the prison by the next day.' Davis tried to turn the tables on Littlewood, hoping that it would give him a chance of escaping with his life.

'Swing in through these gates on your right.' Littlewood cut him short as they had arrived at the industrial estate. Littlewood eased forward in his seat with his gun trained on Davis as he turned in. The estate was a series of small boxy units, four to a block. As they came through the gates, there were four units to their left and four others to their right, with parking bays for half a dozen cars in front of them. Each had roller doors as their main entrance for vehicles, and a small door which led to offices.

'Park over there.' Littlewood gestured with a wave of his gun to a unit at the far end of one block. Davis parked up on one on the bays. Keeping his wits about him, Davis continued with his story, 'When those two kids Thomas Smith and Andrew McNulty were convicted, I heard they got a very warm reception from everybody at Black Lodge Young Offenders. Prisoners and screws alike. And again when they were old enough to be transferred to Claythorn.'

'Thank you for the update, but our little chat has run its course.' With that Littlewood pulled the trigger and put a bullet into Davis's left thigh. Davis screamed in pain as blood flowed out of the wound, soaking his trousers. 'You tortured those sex workers, so that's what I will do to you before . . . well . . . you know . . .'

'That's what you think.' Davis put his foot down hard on the accelerator and aimed the car at the wall in front of them. The car lurched forward and picked up speed. Littlewood was surprised at Davis's actions, but fired one more shot which hit Davis in the left arm before he was thrown back in his seat. Davis's car smashed into the wall at about thirty miles per hour. All the airbags went off, leaving the inside of the car looking like a padded cell.

A groggy and bashed Littlewood sat back up and looked around what was left of the car. Steam was rising from the front, the radiator had split and hot water was spilling out. Bricks from the wall were all over what was left of the bonnet and some were inside because the windscreen had shattered and glass was all over the place. Davis was already half out of the embedded car, trying to make a run for it. But with a bullet in his left arm and thigh, he was struggling. Littlewood, though, dazed from the crash, opened the back door and slid out. Staggering around the back of the Toyota, he saw Davis slumped in pain on the ground. He was clutching his thigh, crying out in pain as blood oozed out. Littlewood stood over Davis. Like a farmer putting an injured animal out of its misery, he fired two more shots into Davis's chest.

'Two down,' Littlewood said under his breath. He stumbled back to the entrance of the industrial estate towards a car parked with its engine running. He opened the door and slumped in, looking straight at the driver.

CHAPTER NINE

Susan turned her little white Renault Clio into the driveway at the front of their house. She turned the engine off, got out and went round to open the passenger door. Putting an arm around her father's back and under his arm, she slowly helped him out of the car. He was groaning from pain with the injuries he'd suffered in the crash.

They'd worked together on the Jackson Davis take out. Susan had dropped her father off near to Austin Lane and pulled into a side street to make sure he was okay and nothing went wrong. They knew Davis frequented red light districts again through their tracking of him over the past few weeks. He'd tried to keep a low profile, using the ones new to the game, and so young they would not have been born when he'd killed before. There were a few of the older ones milling around, still working the streets, who may have recognised him, but he stayed clear of the areas they usually worked.

Austin Lane was a relatively new red light area. It used to be a good residential area, but it had taken a dive after they sold the big houses off and converted them into flats of multiple occupancy. Unsavoury landlords and seedy people moved in and a new community slowly sprung up.

Her father knew which nights Davis liked to go there.

Susan had sat in her car, avoiding the illumination from a nearby street light, with eyes on where her father had taken up position waiting for Davis. She had the radio on down low listening to the local station and its late night music, humming away to the songs she liked, tapping her fingers on the steering wheel.

After about twenty minutes she spotted Davis's car. It pulled up twenty yards away from where she was parked. A petite woman walked over to the car and leaned into the window. Then it all kicked off. She saw her father fly out from where he was standing, shoving the woman out of the way, and jumping into the back seat of Davis's car. A few seconds later the car took off. Susan started the engine and took off after them, nearly sideswiping another parked car as she pulled out. Her car's little engine raced as she tried to keep up. She followed them, keeping a safe distance.

Susan and her father had worked out where they would take Davis – the Barton Industrial Estate, but she was following just in case Davis had other ideas and cocked things up for them. After about fifteen minutes of travelling, she watched them turn into the industrial estate. She passed the gate and turned round, parking opposite the entrance. The road which led into the industrial area was a no-through road and deserted. Some nights, delivery lorries arrived after the units had closed, parking up for the night. She had a good view of where Davis had parked the car.

Susan had gasped when without warning, Davis's car shot forward. The car smashed into the wall in front of them. Susan shouted out in horror as she witnessed what was happening, transfixed on the scene in front of her, unable to move, unable to help her father.

Who'd survived the crash? Davis and not her father? Her father and not Davis? Were they both dead?

Things had gone horribly wrong and she could do nothing about it. After what seemed a long time but in reality was only a few seconds, she saw her father throw open the back door and fall out. He staggered around to the driver's side and two flashes lit up the floor, the car and the wall. Her father stumbled back through the gates and over to where she was parked. He got in, turned to her and whispered, 'Get me home.'

Their next-door neighbour, Mrs Banks, was looking out of her bedroom window as they pulled into their driveway.

'Is he alright, Susan?' she called out in a loud voice, as Susan helped her father out of the car.

'Yes, he's just had a few too many tonight,' Susan replied, helping her father to the door while struggling to find her keys in her pocket.

'Do you need any help? I can get my husband to come down.'

'No, thanks, I can manage.' With that Susan got the front door open and eased her father into the house. She stood him up against the wall and locked the door.

'What did that fucking bitch want?' Littlewood said.

'Dad, that's enough,' Susan said firmly. She guided him down the hall past the lounge and into the kitchen at the back of the house. She eased his arms out of his coat and sat him down at the table.

'Argh, my neck. My arm is killing me,' Littlewood cried out.

'You have whiplash from the crash and you must have bashed your arm against the door when you hit the wall,' Susan explained, as she got a bowl of hot water ready and retrieved the medical box from the back of a kitchen cupboard.

'What the hell happened?' she said, sitting down at

the kitchen table.

'The bastard recognised me,' he said through gritted teeth. Half through the pain he was in, half through annoyance and frustration. He slammed the hand of his good right arm onto the table. The few items on the tabletop jumped with the ferocity.

'What? How?' Susan said, staring at her father in bewilderment.

Littlewood spent the next half hour telling her every detail of his conversation with Jackson Davis, in-between the shouts of pain and curses as Susan tended to his wounds and strains. When she'd finished and dosed him up with painkillers it was almost 1 a.m. Susan led her still-shaken father through the hall and up the stairs to his bedroom, picking up his coat on the way. She helped to undress him and made sure he was comfortable in bed, then sat on the edge.

'I want you to lie low for a few days. You need to gain your strength and recover from this,' Susan reproached.

He knew it was no good arguing with her.

'You've almost risked everything in taking down Jackson Davis, including your life. And I don't like it. It was stupid and careless. The police will be all over this from now on, and we need to be careful in what we do and how we do it.'

Littlewood smiled, 'You're right.' He winced. The painkillers had not kicked in yet.

'I know I'm right,' Susan replied. 'Good night Dad.' Susan kissed her father on his forehead and got up.

She went over to his coat on a nearby chair, removed the gun from the pocket and stared at it. Then, opening his wardrobe she took out the rucksack, put the gun in it, and took out the red book. Opening it, she put a line through the name of Jackson Davis. She looked at the other names her father had on the list, smiling to herself as she returned the book to the rucksack and returned it to the wardrobe.

CHAPTER TEN

THURSDAY MORNING

Watson and Monteith arrived at the Barton Industrial Estate after being diverted there from their way to the station. After showing their IDs to the Police Constable assigned to guard the gate, they were directed toward the crashed car. Just inside the gate, a group of about a hundred members of the public were gathered behind a section of crime tape. Most of them workers from some of the industrial units who had turned up for a normal day's work, only to find today would not be a normal day.

'Ladies and gentleman,' Monteith burst out as they went past them. 'Here are the finest detectives in the city, Keith Monteith and Terry Watson, hurray.' Monteith added a mock wave. Watson tried not to laugh but failed miserably.

Monteith parked up, and they surveyed the scene as they got out. What was left of the Toyota was imbedded in a wall of one of the units. The rear-left passenger door was open, as was the driver's door. By the driver's door a white tent covered a body. Mac was busy buzzing around the tent and two forensic technicians were taking pictures of the inside of the car. By another of the industrial units, uniformed officers were taking statements from two people, who looked like they worked there.

'Morning boys. What a lovely day.' Mac was in the back of his van as they approached the car.

'I swear you love your job too much,' Monteith joked. 'Why are we here? Is it not just an abandoned crashed car?'

'Body under the tent has four bullet holes in him. My guess 9mm. Will find out when I get him back to the morgue.'

After they had put on protective shoe coverings and gloves, Max held back the tent opening for them to enter. Jackson Davis was on his back. His glazed eyes half-open. His chest was dark red with the blood from the two bullet holes. Blood had also pooled under his left side from the wounds to his leg and arm.

'Thanks Mac, we've seen enough,' Watson said, as he followed the trail of blood which led from where Davis lay under the tent to the driver's door. He looked in through the door. Blood was all over the front seats and down by the gear stick. He couldn't see much due to the airbags deploying in the car, the broken windscreen, the bricks, and the crumpled dashboard. Monteith joined him. 'Certainly no accident, but what happened first? The shots in the leg and arm, or the crash?' Watson mused. 'The chest shots were definitely fired from outside the car. There's not enough room in the back of the car to do them.'

'Hopefully one of these units has working CCTV that will show something,' Monteith pondered. 'I'll get one of the PCs to ask around.'

He turned to Mac. 'See you later in the morgue for your update.' Mac waved in their general direction as he continued to gather evidence.

'Detectives?' one of the PCs who was gathering statements, called them. Watson and Monteith turned and walked across to see what he had found. 'This is Mr

Holland. He found the car and body.'

Mr Holland was dressed in blue work overalls and steel toe-capped boots. He explained that his unit housed a small engineering business.

'I arrived about 7.30 a.m. as normal. I saw the crashed car as I came through the gates. I thought a joy rider had left it there. We get a few cars like that, some smashed up, and some burned out. It was not until I got closer that I saw the body. I rang the police as soon as I unlocked my unit.'

'Did you go near the car or touch anything before the police arrived?' Watson said.

'No,' Holland said emphatically. 'Me and a couple of others went round as people arrived, telling them to keep back, not only because of the body, but also because the unit could be unsafe.'

Watson nodded. 'Did you see anyone else in the area, hanging around either on foot or in a car you did not recognise?'

Holland shook his head. 'No. Only the regular cars owned by the workers here who come in around the same time as me.'

Before Watson had a chance to ask more questions, there was a commotion over where the public were kept back. Bursting through was a man in a suit and tie. He was walking purposely over to the crime scene. Two of the PCs were trying, and failing, to stop him.

'What the fuck is happening? Why are we being stopped from entering the estate and working?' he shouted as he made his way across the tarmac.

'Excuse me, Sir,' Watson held his hand out in a stop signal as he met the man coming towards them. 'Who are you?'

'It does not matter who I am, why are we being stopped?'

'I heard you the first time, as did everyone around

here,' Watson said. 'Again, I would like to know who you are?'

'The name is McGill, James McGill if you really need to know. I own some of the businesses here, and you are stopping me from getting my deliveries out. Time is money don't you know.'

He was a large chap. Watson had seen it all before. Men acting with bravado because of their size. The bigger they are, the harder they fall he reminded himself, before responding with a measured tone.

'Well, excuse me Mr McGill. We have a crime scene here and until we have finished, I'm afraid that this estate will remain closed. Please, can you return to behind the tape?'

'What! For a car which some little joy-riding prick crashed. Haven't you got better things to do?' McGill was indignant with rage.

With that, Watson lost his cool. 'Let me fucking show you,' he bellowed in McGill's face. He grabbed McGill by the scruff of his collar and dragged him around the car to where Jackson Davis's body was.

'Hey what are you doing? Get the fuck off of me,' McGill stammered. Watson flung back the flaps of the tent and shoved McGill in, following right behind.

'Does this look like a joy-riding prick to you? Well?'

Mac and his partner were sealing up the body bag to transport Davis's body back to the morgue. McGill could only see the top half of Davis, but it was enough. He gasped and gulped, ran out of the tent and threw up on the ground. After he had tidied himself up, Watson was waiting for him. Standing face-to-face with him, he lowered his voice.

'Piss off back behind the tape, or I will arrest you for obstruction of a crime scene. Do you understand?'

McGill nodded nervously. Still feeling nauseous he wandered off, muttering under his breath.

Mac appeared at Watson's shoulder watching McGill trying to regain his composure in front of everyone standing nearby. 'Interesting policing,' he commented, glancing down at the pile of vomit that McGill had left. 'Good job forensics have finished, or they would curse you for contaminating the area.'

Back in the car, Monteith had a smirk on his face. They were driving back to the station, following the private ambulance which carried the body of Davis back to Mac's morgue.

'What?' Watson glanced at Monteith.

'I was wondering, when did they teach us what you just did at police training, because I can't have been in class that day. Either I was ill or in bed with that blonde called Carol.'

'Oh, piss off!' Watson replied. They burst out laughing. When it died down Watson queried, 'You and Carol?'

Monteith smirked again. 'Just a little homework with handcuffs.'

They laughed again.

Their laughing stopped, and the smiles were wiped off their faces when they entered their office in the station.

CHAPTER ELEVEN

'Monteith, Watson, get in here,' Crompton bellowed from his office doorway as soon as he saw them. He was not alone. Detective Superintendent Grant Matthews was waiting for them too.

Lorimer leaned back in his chair and smiled as they went past. 'Do you want to borrow my riot gear?'

Watson smiled back and gave him the finger.

When they got to his office, Crompton was sitting behind his desk looking pissed off, and the superintendent was standing ramrod straight looking out of the window. DSI Matthews's uniform was immaculate with creases so sharp they could cut glass. His black hair looked like someone had painted it on, not one hair out of place. His shoes shone so much they gleamed.

Watson and Monteith didn't even get into Crompton's office before Matthews turned and started his rant. 'What the hell did you think you were doing?'

'Pardon?' Watson looked blank as he came through the door.

Everyone outside stopped what they were doing and listened in on the argument.

'You know exactly what I am on about. That stunt you pulled at the industrial estate. I have had a very irate and angry James McGill on the phone. He said you assaulted him,' Matthews continued.

'The jerk wouldn't get out of the way, and was acting as if he owned the place,' Watson tried to explain.

Matthews was in no mood for explanations and he continued his rant pointing his finger at Watson. 'That is no excuse. I had to calm McGill down, because he was talking about making it official. I talked him down and around and finally out of it, but you are lucky he is not taking this further.'

'I'm lucky? He's lucky that he's not sitting in a jail cell,' Watson argued back.

'Enough. Kenneth, get your detectives in order or they will be back on beat duty before they know it.' With that Matthews grabbed his hat off the desk and threw open the door. He marched out into the main office, his face like thunder. Everyone out there averted their gaze and busied themselves to avoid eye contact.

Before they could ask what just happened, Crompton put his hand up, got up from his desk and closed the door.

'How the hell did Matthews get involved?' a stunned Monteith said.

Crompton sat back at his desk. 'Because it's not what you know, but who you know. McGill and Matthews know each other from the golf club.'

'But McGill behaved like a dickhead. Terry's right, we could have arrested him.'

'And he would have been out before you completed your paperwork. McGill may be a dickhead, but he is a dickhead with connections. Connections that control all of us.' Crompton sighed. 'But . . . I must admit I wish I had been there to see what you did.' Crompton's face lit up with a big grin and the laughter returned.

'Okay, so what do we know about what happened with this crashed car and the body?' Crompton said, as they moved back into the main office.

Lorimer brought them up to speed.

'Just to backtrack on Freeman, the door-to-door visits came up with nothing. And when we tracked his cellmates, most are still in prison and those who have been released have left the area. As for last night, the car, according to the DVLA, belongs to a Jackson Davis – address Manor Street, recently released from Claythorn Prison.'

'Another ex-prisoner, two in two days. Coincidence?' Monteith said out loud.

Nobody responded, all pondering over the question.

'What was he in for?' Crompton said.

Lorimer continued. 'They jailed him for the torture and killing of two sex workers twenty-five years ago. He was released on licence six months ago.'

'Okay,' Monteith said. 'We have two ex-prisoners both jailed for killing people, both shot dead months after coming out. Do we have a serial killer?'

Everyone looked at each other, contemplating the huge impact on the city if it was.

'Apart from the fact they were both in jail it seems a bit of a tentative link. How many get released each year from prison, thousands? And because two get shot in two days there's a nutter running loose? What do we do, stop them releasing prisoners?' Watson said dismissively.

'No, but I think it's something we should think about,' Crompton cut in.

Monteith continued, 'Somebody must have held a grudge for a long time in that case, which is doubtful. Freeman was in for what . . . twelve years, Davis for twenty-five. No I don't buy it.'

'Buying or not, let's concentrate on the things we can deal with. Lorimer, you take two other officers and go to Davis's address. See if he has any family and talk to the neighbours. Keith, Terry, both of you go and see if Mac has started on Davis's autopsy.'

-X-

Monteith parked in the private bays around the back of the city hospital reserved for Mac's mortuary. The sign on the wall said Bereavement Care Centre. As they entered through a set of double doors and walked down into the clinically clean anteroom, they heard the blasting music coming from Mac's morgue before they'd even pushed open the frosted glass door to the sound of AC/DC's classic *Highway to Hell*.

Mac was sitting at his desk, going through a pile of files, singing at the top of his voice. He looked up to see the pair of detectives head banging and playing air guitar.

'You two look like right pillocks!' he said, bursting out laughing as he reached over to turn the music off. 'Bon Scott would turn in his grave.'

'That's loud enough to wake the dead!' Monteith responded, shaking his head trying to regain his hearing. 'And who the hell is or was Bon Scott?'

'Ronald Belford 'Bon' Scott was the original singer of AC/DC, who unfortunately took his own highway to hell back in 1980.' Mac enjoyed recounting rock-and-roll history to anyone who would listen.

'We have great sing-a-longs down here, me and my mates,' Mac said, going over to the freezer drawers. He opened one. 'Jane Doe here has got a wicked voice.'

'You're nuts Mac. So what are these two, backing singers?' Watson was pointing to the two covered bodies on the tables.

'No. These are fresh in today. Couple killed in a head-on collision with a lorry. Driver fell asleep at the wheel. They didn't stand a chance. I was just going over the paperwork before examining them. Want to stay and watch?' Mac picked up a scalpel and a hacksaw from the table of instruments, looking at them longingly as if they were his pride and joys, which they, in fact, were.

'No fear. You couldn't even pay me to watch you do your stuff. It's bad enough looking at the bodies at a crime scene,' Monteith said adamantly, as he backed away to the door.

Watson took over. 'Okay Mac, before Keith faints or does something else, we came down to see if you had anything on Jackson Davis. Have you examined him yet?'

'Nope. He is being prepped by my colleague in the other room. As you can gather, we are rather busy at the moment. Would you gentlemen like to come through here so I can introduce you to the late Mr Davis?'

Mac opened the swinging doors to the adjacent room, holding them open for the detectives to follow.

'I think I will wait here Mac, I can see perfectly well from here,' Monteith said, as he came through the door and spotted the covered body on the aluminium table.

'Feeling squeamish are we?' Mac tried to goad him.

'No! I will . . . stay here.'

'Okay. Terry, you all right with this?'

'Yep, let's see him.'

Mac approached the table and pulled the sheet off Davis's naked body. 'Right. We have four bullet wounds. Looking at the ones on the upper leg, here, and the arm above the elbow, here, the angle of the wounds suggests that the killer was sitting behind him on the back seat. The two in the chest were fired outside the car. Judging by the angle of them, the killer was standing above him and firing down. The broken ribs, cuts and bruises to the chest, legs and head came from the crash.'

'Are the bullets still in him?' Watson said.

'No. I've already taken them out and given them to ballistics,' Mac said as he turned and picked up another scalpel. 'Sure you won't stay?'

Hearing the doors fly open, Mac and Watson both spun around catching Monteith flying out.

'I think I'll pass. Looks like I've a detective to catch.'

-X-

Lorimer and two female Police Constables arrived in a squad car at Davis's house in Manor Street, taking in the surrounding area. The park across the road was busy, the traffic on the road light. They walked up the drive towards the house, noticing the curtains were drawn. As they approached, there was movement behind the curtains downstairs as the head of an Alsatian poked through. It barked nonstop from when it saw them until they arrived at the front door.

'Oh, what a lovely dog,' one Police Constable said. 'My parents own an Alsatian called Buster.'

Lorimer looked at her. 'You say that now when we're safe outside the house. Let's see what you think when we get in.' He knocked hard on the front door. The Alsatian flew at the door, banging it, barking loudly, defending its territory.

'Is it still a lovely dog now?' Lorimer turned and smiled at her.

'Hello? Excuse me?' An old gentleman was walking up the driveway, waving. He was dressed in a shirt and cardigan with smart trousers and dark shoes.

Lorimer turned and walked towards him. 'Can I help you?'

'I'm sorry; my name is Donald Carter. I saw your car from my house next door. Are you after Jackson Davis?' the neighbour said.

'Do you know Mr Davis well?' Lorimer said.

'Not personally. I spoke more with his parents. Nice couple. Jackson keeps to himself. Weird man. When he was jailed for those murders his parents never got over

51

it. It was a big shock for them.'

'When did you last see Mr Davis?' Lorimer pulled out his notebook.

'Let me see. I remember last night seeing his car at about 9.30 p.m. But when I looked out around 10 p.m. before I went to bed, it wasn't here.'

'Okay, thank you for that.' Lorimer jotted it down. 'There is no answer from the house. Have you seen his parents? We need to talk to them.'

'You will have a job doing that. His father died about four years ago. Cancer, very quick. His mother is in a home. Jackson had to put her there about three months ago for her own safety. Alzheimer's. Poor woman doesn't know what day it is half the time. The wife and I looked after her after his father died, and before he came out.' Lorimer was noting it down, having trouble keeping up.

He turned to one Police Constable. 'We will need a locksmith and a dog warden.'

She nodded and disappeared towards the squad car to make the arrangements.

'Why are you doing that? I'm sure Mr Davis will be back later.' Carter looked worried.

'I'm sorry to say, but Mr Davis was involved in an accident last night. I'm afraid he has died,' Lorimer informed the neighbour.

'Oh God, oh no. How terrible,' Carter exclaimed, paling.

Lorimer beckoned the other Police Constable over. 'Can you take him back to his, and stay with him until he is okay?'

She led the neighbour away, leaving Lorimer with his thoughts.

He had never been involved with a major murder enquiry before. Prior to this secondment he was in charge of the outlying police stations dealing with delegating work, supervising investigations, monitoring law enforcement operations, supervising responses to critical incidents and managing resources. Now building up to his National Investigators Exam to become a detective, this was his big chance to impress, and he was looking forward to doing just that.

CHAPTER TWELVE

SATURDAY

A couple of days had passed before Littlewood felt he was well enough to venture out.

Maybe a visit to his wife's grave. But it came with Susan's strict ruling that he was only to go there and back, not to try and do anything else. She was worried that he would start looking for another person on his list, and he was not mentally or physically fit enough for that yet.

He called in on the florist's first for some flowers to put on the grave. Red roses, Jackie's favourites. They had grown them in both the front and back garden at their house. Jackie was always outside, tending to them, dead heading, spraying, and keeping the weeds down. Littlewood smiled sadly at the memory of his late wife. Parking his Škoda in the small car park outside the local council cemetery and collecting the roses off the back seat, he entered through the large gates.

The sun was shining bright, and as it filtered through the leaves on the trees it left a dappled look on the paths. There were a couple of other people visiting their loved ones. A fresh grave was being dug in a far corner of the already overcrowded cemetery. Reaching Jackie's granite headstone, he knelt down and placed the roses against it. He slowly traced his hand over the inscription as he always did.

Her Life A Beautiful Memory, Her Absence A Silent Grief.

After a mumbled prayer, he got up and sat on a nearby bench, gathering his thoughts. His mind drifted back to when he first saw Jackie, at the local sixth-form college. They had attended different secondary schools prior to sixth form. Colin leaving with ten O-Levels, Jackie with eight. Soon they became inseparable, spending as much time together as they could. He remembered their first holidays together. Non-parent holidays. Nothing extravagant like jetting off to Ibiza or the Canary Islands, more B&B holidays on the rain and sun-drenched coast of Britain, walking along cliff paths. Exploring off-the-beaten-track villages and secluded beaches.

University was never on the cards for either of them, so they got jobs working for local firms saving money for a deposit on their first flat. They were married soon after Jackie's 20th birthday. Eleven months later Susan arrived.

Colin started working at Claythorn Prison as a prison officer, and they moved into the house they were to call home. It should have been the whole of their life, well into retirement, but twelve years of marriage to his childhood sweetheart had ended that one night, ten years ago.

A wife, a mother, and a friend, taken from him and his daughter.

There could have been two people in that grave if they had not allowed Susan, who was ten years old back then, to have a sleepover at a friend's. He had been on a night shift at Claythorn Prison.

On his way into work he had dropped a very excitable Susan at her friend's. The shift had been as uneventful as it could be until his boss had called him into the wing office. An hour later he was at his wife's bedside in the hospital's emergency ward crying inconsolably. She was on a life support system with severe head injuries, a broken arm and two broken ribs.

He was told by the police that his next-door neighbour Mr Banks, who was giving his dog a late-night walk, saw two teenagers running out of the back gate of the Littlewoods' house, nearly knocking him over in their effort to get away. Mr Banks went inside through the open back door, and he found Jackie unconscious at the bottom of the stairs. Blood was pouring from a head wound. He had called 999 straight away.

The police and an ambulance arrived soon after, rushing Jackie to hospital and securing the house. Judging by the mess the house was in, the two teenagers had been in the process of ransacking it when Littlewood's wife had disturbed them. She had either been pushed or fallen down the stairs.

With the description given by Banks, and the fingerprints left at the scene, Thomas Smith and Andrew McNulty were arrested three days later. Charged with burglary and initially, GBH with intent. They upgraded the charges to murder when Jackie succumbed to her injuries a week later.

At the trial, both Smith and McNulty pleaded guilty to burglary, but not to murder. The jury found them not guilty of murder, but guilty of manslaughter. A murder charge could not be reached because the jury couldn't decide if Jackie had slipped and fallen down the stairs or was pushed. Smith and McNulty each received ten years.

In the intervening years, Littlewood found himself in a very dark place. Depression set in. A wrestle with the Black Dog. Drink also became a good friend.

Littlewood tried to go back to work following months off with his depression. When he was at work he either smelled of booze or arrived drunk. The end came when he was disciplined for hitting a prisoner who goaded him over his wife's death. Littlewood was medically discharged from the prison service soon after.

It was then he started to formulate a plan to get his own back.

CHAPTER THIRTEEN

MONDAY

Littlewood parked up at the end of a long tree-lined lane. Along one side were fourteen poplar trees, stretching so high it looked like they were almost touching the sky. Behind them, the fields were planted with various crops.

On the other side of the lane were large fancy houses and country retreats big enough to hold parties without disturbing the neighbours. They were an estate agent's gold mine. If your company bagged selling one on the odd occasion one came up for sale, you'd be quids in on commission.

The lane was on the edge of a little village, five miles to the north of West Ravenswood. It was a picture-postcard view in spring and summer, but a pain to get out of during winter snowfalls.

Littlewood was looking at the house at the very end of the lane. Number 10, also called Horizons. He had been here before with Jackie. But that was in better times. They used to be invited to the numerous parties there by the owner and his wife. Team building the owner used to call it. Drunken revelries would be a better description of the nights' events.

Littlewood alighted from his car and walked the few metres to the entrance of the driveway. Two brick pillars with large granite balls on top, leading to a brick-laid driveway large enough for five or six cars. Only one was parked at the moment, a brand-new Mercedes C-Class. Well-kept holly hedges bordered the front garden. The house had a stunning Tudor-style frontage.

He knocked on the front door twice but no answer came. Littlewood walked away down the side of the house, with the detached double garage to his left. He could hear the sound of a lawn mower as he opened the side gate leading to the vast back garden. A swimming pool was in front of the patio doors. Beyond that, a huge lawn surrounded by large shrubs and trees. Riding on a sit-on lawnmower was the owner of this grand house, the person Littlewood was there to see.

Retired prison governor Adrian Knowles reached the far end of the lawn, turned the lawnmower around and headed back towards the house. He looked up and noticed the man standing on his patio. Littlewood waved as he saw Knowles coming towards the house. Knowles parked up by the patio and turned the lawnmower off.

'Can I help you? How did you get in here?' Knowles was puzzled as he walked towards the intruder.

'It's me. Colin Littlewood.'

'Colin? Oh yes I remember, from Claythorn.' Knowles seemed to remember but was still unsure. 'How long has it been?' He held out his hand for Littlewood to shake.

'Eight years since Claythorn. Ten years since Jackie.' Littlewood's voice still cracked a bit. He found talking about his late wife hard even after all these years.

'That long! I didn't realise it was so long ago. Since I retired from the service one day rolls into another. How is your daughter? Susan isn't it?'

'She has coped okay, better than me in some ways. She has her bad days and weeks. She's working now as an administration manager at a local firm.'

'Wow, you must be proud of her. And you? How are you doing? Are you working?'

Knowles had visibly relaxed and looked more at ease with his visitor. Littlewood's little history cameo was working.

'That's why I came to see you. I need help in getting back into the job market. I have had a couple of short-lived jobs since the service but I was hoping you could help?'

Knowles rubbed his chin thinking, 'Erm, I don't know.'

'I can see you are busy. I was wrong to just turn up, I'm sorry,' Littlewood said as humbly as he could, turning from Knowles as if to walk away. Knowles reached out and put a hand on Littlewood's shoulder.

'No . . . no don't go. Please come inside and we will talk and see what we can come up with. After what you went through, it's the least I can do.'

He led the way through the patio doors into the large living room. Two wine-coloured three-seater sofas dominated the room, facing each other with a glass topped wooden coffee table between them. A landscape picture hung over an open fire. A sixty-inch plasma screen television with surround-sound hung on the opposite wall. At the far end of the room, a six-seated dining room table.

They went on into the kitchen, surprisingly small for such a big house.

Knowles picked up the kettle. 'Tea or coffee?'

'Neither,' Littlewood replied.

Knowles swung round to find Littlewood standing in the doorway with a gun aimed at him.

'Colin? What is this?'

'Sit down!' Littlewood said.

Knowles put the kettle down and slowly sat down on one of the wooden chairs at the kitchen table, his eyes flicking between the gun and Littlewood's face.

'Colin, whatever it is I'm sure we can work something out.'

Littlewood approached the table with hate in his eyes. 'Too late for that. I needed help ten years ago, but got nothing. My wife was murdered, and I got no help.'

This was personal. Freeman and Davis had been nothing to Littlewood, just scum who needed dealing with.

'No help?' Knowles shouted, 'We gave you a lot of help. As much time off as you needed. Close to six months wasn't it? We arranged bereavement counselling.'

'Counselling! Is that what you called it? The counsellor needed more help than I did.' Littlewood's anger was approaching a dangerously high level.

Knowles tried to take the tension out of the situation. 'We put you on shifts to help you look after Susan. Not putting you back on the wings so you could settle back into work. If I remember, you were in the prisoner reception area when you came back. You only had to work days and no weekends. We were all happy for you and Susan when McNulty and Smith got what they deserved.'

Littlewood screamed back in Knowles's face. 'They murdered Jackie. They should have got more, but that sodding jury were conned by the so-called evidence.' Littlewood lost it and hit Knowles over the head with the gun. And again. Blood started to poor down Knowles's face. Knowles rubbed the blood away from his eyes and nose as he tried to speak.

'But then you ruined everything, including your career, by turning up for work drunk, or missing your shifts altogether. And putting Freeman in the hospital with a broken nose was the final straw. I couldn't protect you after that.'

Littlewood's mind went back to that fateful day.

One of the few days he was sober enough to go to work. The prisoner reception area was where the newcomers to the prison had to relinquish their possessions and outside clothing before being given their prison clothes. Officers oversaw this, but serving prisoners could work in there as a privilege if they had behaved. One of those inmates that day was Ronald Freeman.

Littlewood, although sober, had been in a foul mood, giving grief to anyone around him. There had been six newcomers that day. As Freeman was handing out clothes to a newcomer, Littlewood shouted at him to hurry up and pushed him out of the way. Freeman gave back a verbal volley about the death of Littlewood's wife. Littlewood lost it and replied with two swift punches to Freeman's face before being restrained by his colleagues. Freeman landed in the hospital wing with a busted nose, and Littlewood ended up being sacked for gross misconduct.

Knowles, sensing that Littlewood was not paying full attention started to get out of his chair. 'Colin, please. Let's try to work something out. I can help you get what you need.'

'I don't need help from you.' Littlewood quickly fired two shots into Knowles's chest. Knowles staggered backwards and fell up against the kitchen side, sliding down onto the floor, blood pooling around his body.

Putting the gun into his jacket pocket, Littlewood turned and walked out of the kitchen and back into the living room. He looked out of the patio windows, making sure the neighbours were not around.

Quickly, he made his way back to his car through the side gate and down the driveway. Opening his car door, he slumped into the seat. Emotion that had built up during the argument with Knowles rushed out of him and he burst into floods of tears. It took a lot out of him, thinking about his wife, and killing Knowles, once a colleague and friend.

-X-

Susan arrived at her place of work at 8.45 a.m., parking her Renault Clio in the employees' car park.

The morning sun was so bright; she kept her sunglasses on while walking towards the main door. Other staff were talking between themselves of what they had done during the weekend, and muttering about the workday ahead.

The main reception area was purposely unwelcoming. All the floors and walls had grey tiles. The reception desk was behind security glass and always manned by two people. CCTV cameras had been placed both inside and outside of the main door. No personal effects were allowed to be taken through into work areas. Employees had to put their belongings into lockers before entering.

Susan showed her ID to the reception staff and was buzzed through the sets of doors leading to her office. She walked along the carpeted corridor, called into the mail room, and picked up a pile of files. She put the files down on her office desk and searched through them for two in particular. Once found, she opened her handbag and brought out two pieces of photocopied paper.

She inserted one in each file and then put the files back in with the others.

CHAPTER FOURTEEN

Trying to get three kids out of bed, washed, dressed and fed on a school day was akin to military action in the Watson home.

Simon and Jason were first as they always left before the others. Simon was in year seven at South Meadows Academy. Jason was in the last year at the local primary. With both schools being next to each other, they walked together. Sally, a teacher at the primary school, took Rachel in with her.

As Watson was polishing off toast and coffee while watching BBC's *Breakfast*, his phone went off – breaking the tedium of wars, politics and so-called celebrities at glitzy parties. It was Monteith, and he was not happy.

'Can you pick me up today? I have car problems.'

'Yes, sure. What's up with your pride and joy?'

'You will see when you get here.' With that Monteith had gone.

Watson looked at his phone, confused. He turned the television off and took his mug and plate into the kitchen.

'Who was on the phone?' Sally said. She was getting Rachel ready by the front door, putting her coat on.

'Keith. He wants me to drive today. Says he has car

problems, but wouldn't say what.'

'He's probably only got it dirty and didn't want to be seen out in it. I swear he spends more time with that car than with Katie and the kids,' Sally said with disdain. 'We are off now. Come on Rachel.'

Rachel ran and wrapped her arms around her dad's legs, then skipped out through the front door with her bag strapped to her back.

'He's not that bad. I would be careful if I had a car like his.'

'There's careful and then there's neurotic. And he borders on being neurotic over that car,' Sally replied, on her way out of the door.

Watson pulled into the street where Monteith lived. His car was being loaded onto the back of a recovery vehicle. Monteith and his wife Katie were having a full-blown argument in the front garden. Their children, ten-year-old Rebecca and five-year-old Pixie, were looking out of the lounge window.

Watson jumped out of his car and raced over. He looked at the car being loaded and noticed that it had had all of its tyres slashed. 'What the hell happened?'

'Ask him!' Katie bellowed. 'He's fucked everything up,' she said, storming into the house and slamming the front door behind her.

'What does she mean?' Watson said in bewilderment.

'It's nothing,' Monteith replied dismissively.

'Nothing? Katie's running around screaming at you. Your car has its tyres slashed, and you're saying it's nothing. What the hell has happened?'

Monteith walked passed Watson. 'Let's get out of here. I need breakfast.'

Twenty minutes later, Monteith was tucking into a full English. They had driven in silence to the cafe near to their headquarters.

'So are you going to tell me what happened back there?' Watson kept his voice low. The cafe was packed with customers. Some of the beat coppers were in there, winding down, going over what had happened during their night shifts.

'The car is a warning,' Monteith said between mouthfuls.

'A warning? From who?'

Monteith stopped eating, 'Jimmy Russell.'

'Russell? What have you done to enrage that lunatic?' Watson tried to keep his anger in check and his voice low as a waitress came by the table. 'Russell is not one to get on the wrong side of. You should know that.'

Monteith slurped his tea and then stared down into the cup, avoiding Terry's eyes. 'I owe him money. Gambling debts.'

'How much do you owe?' Watson said warily, as if hesitant to know the answer.

'Five grand.'

'You owe one of the biggest crooks in West Ravenswood five grand?! You fucking idiot. Do you have a death wish?'

Watson got up and stormed out of the cafe. Monteith just looked at him in stunned silence, his fork halfway to his mouth. Other customers were looking over. Monteith put his fork down and wiped his mouth, composing himself. 'Have you not seen a domestic before?' he called out to the cafe residents, then walked out.

Watson was sitting in his car, with the engine running. His face still contorted with anger. Monteith slowly got into the passenger seat.

'You need to get yourself sorted.' Watson stared straight ahead out of the windscreen. 'You almost fucked up your marriage before it began with your gambling. And judging by Katie this morning, you are well on the way to doing it again.'

'She will be fine,' Monteith replied, acting as if nothing was wrong and it was perfectly normal.

'Fine? Fine! It's a wonder she's not ripped your balls off. Listen to yourself. You have a family to look after now. Think about them for once.'

Watson pulled out into the traffic and headed for their headquarters. 'We are already looking for one murderous psychopath. I don't want to go looking for another one in Russell because something has happened to you.'

CHAPTER FIFTEEN

The office was deciphering what the newspapers, both local and national, were saying about the shootings. Putting two and two together and making five. Sensationalism as only newspapers can pull off, even though they had the official statement put out by the Police Press Office.

'It's amazing how the press can link the two shootings together, when we've told them we haven't done so,' Crompton expressed, throwing one paper down angrily.

He had just got his ear chewed off by Matthews who insisted the two killings were linked. 'Why haven't we made a breakthrough yet?' Matthews had demanded.

An exasperated Crompton had replied, 'Sir, we have found nothing to link them. One was in a pub car park, and the other at an industrial estate. Yes, both were shootings, but that's all. The newspapers love to hype a story up to sell more, but they know squat. They're just guessing.'

But Matthews had pressed on before demanding to be kept up to date and disappearing.

Crompton brought the office to order. 'Okay, give me some good news.'

Lorimer began by filling everybody in on the visit to Jackson Davis's home, and the conversation with the neighbour Mr Carter. 'Now we know Davis went out between 9.30 and 10 p.m. on the night he died. We need to look at CCTV to see where he went and who he met.'

'Right, as you found out about Davis, you can have the lovely job of trawling through the CCTV images. We've already asked for the discs covering last Wednesday and they arrived over the weekend. They're all yours.' Crompton smiled.

'That's all right. I'm used to box set marathons. I watched the whole of *Breaking Bad* the other weekend,' Lorimer laughed, getting out of his chair. 'And lads, just remember to bring me lots of coffee.'

He reappeared after three hours of trawling through the CCTV pictures, looking like the cat that got the cream. Crompton called them into a side room which had a large screen so they could see the relevant images in greater detail.

'Where's the popcorn?' Monteith joked, as they sat down.

'Shut up and concentrate,' Crompton shot back. 'Lorimer, the floor is yours.'

'Thank you, Sir.' Lorimer was sat at the computer ready to show them what he had found. 'We know Davis left his house between 9.30 and 10 p.m. last Wednesday night. That information we got from the neighbour. It was difficult tracking his car at first because of its dark colour, but thanks to the Automatic Number Plate Recognition system I have got more information. These first few pictures show Davis's car traveling on the duel carriageway on the outskirts of the city between 10.40 and 11 p.m. We see Davis then exiting the junction that leads to the Barton Industrial Estate. CCTV coverage is patchy on the estate so there are no clear pictures we can use.'

Monteith's phone went off as Lorimer continued. 'Just going to take this,' Monteith said, getting out of his chair.

'No, you're not, sit down,' Crompton barked.

Monteith mumbled something as he sat back, causing Crompton to scowl at him.

Lorimer continued. 'The city centre pictures were difficult to pick out with the volume of traffic and not knowing where he was going. The first time we have him after leaving his house is on Crane Street heading into Bankside at 10.05 p.m.' He put up the next picture. 'The next time we see him was close to Austin Lane at 10.20 p.m.'

'Austin Lane, interesting,' Crompton sounded quizzical.

'I lost him for a time around this area, but I picked him up leaving and heading out of the city around 10.35 p.m.' Lorimer put up the next picture, a close up of Davis's car, and stood by the screen. 'If you look closer there is Davis, and there could be someone in the back of the car, but I can't be certain.' There was a black shape in the back but it was unrecognisable.

'Thank you,' Crompton walked over to the screen not taking his eyes off the last picture. 'As you well know, Austin Lane is the newest of the red light areas which are blighting this city. Davis looked like he had started to visit these areas again.'

'You would think he would have kept his head down after being released. Six months later and he's back at it,' Watson said.

'He's just sticking two fingers up at the justice system. You will not change people like Davis, and in all my time on the force I have seen many like him.'

'If he was done over by a pimp, or a prostitute, that would be some kind of justice,' Monteith added looking at his phone.

Crompton noticed but continued, 'Well, we need to find out what happened around Austin Lane. Who did he meet? Did anybody see him or his car? Anyone fancy some overtime tonight over at Austin Lane? We need to do this before it goes cold.'

Lorimer and Watson both said they would. Monteith was looking at his phone until Watson nudged him. 'What, yes I will.'

'Okay, I will let you know the details later. Thanks.'

As everyone was leaving the room, Crompton called out, 'Keith, my office, now!'

Crompton led the way, shutting the door after Monteith entered.

'What the hell was that with your phone?'

'I was waiting for a call,' Monteith tried to explain.

'What? You think a personal call is more important than this investigation? More important to answer that call while we were going through information which could lead to a breakthrough?'

'Somebody slashed all the tyres on my car last night. The call was from the garage.'

'Whatever you have going on in your private life, you keep it separate from your work. Got it? Good. Get back out there. You *are* going to Austin Lane tonight, car tyres or no car tyres.'

Monteith stormed straight past everyone, out of the office. Watson looked at Lorimer. 'I'd best check on him.'

Out in the corridor, Monteith was on his phone arguing with the garage. 'Yes, yes, how much?! You are joking. Okay, I will pick it up later.' Monteith turned round to see Watson. 'Five hundred for four tyres, the robbing gits.'

'Did you tell Crompton about what happened?' Watson said.

'Only about the tyres, not about the other thing. He

made it perfectly clear not to mix private life with work.'

'Get your head on straight before we go back in there.' Watson tried to calm Monteith down. 'I will drop you off to pick up your car and then we'll get Austin Lane sorted. Okay?'

Monteith agreed, but when they came back into the office, things had developed even more. And not for the better.

'Right, gather around,' said Crompton. 'Change of plan. I just got a phone call. There has been another shooting, over at Bennington this time. Watson, Monteith, I want you to check that out. Mac and his team are already at the house. Here is the address. Lorimer, looks like I'm coming with you tonight to Austin Lane. Let's get going.'

-X-

It was almost evening when they got to Bennington. Monteith had picked his car up, so they arrived separately. 'Hope this doesn't take too long,' Monteith grumbled.

'Got some place to be? More important than this?' Watson threw him a look.

The driveway of the house had already been taped off. Mac's morgue van and the Crime Scene Investigation vehicle were parked on it. The front door was covered with a forensic tent. After signing in, they took a mask, paper shoes and gloves out of the boxes next to the door, and slipped them on over their Tyvek coveralls. Inside the house the forensic team was busy collecting evidence. Watson and Monteith stood in front of the house where they could see through into the main living room. The forensic technicians had also erected a tent over the patio doors. More of the crime scene investigators were taking photographs of the patio area and dusting for fingerprints.

'Mac?' Watson called out seeing him crouched on the kitchen floor over the body of a male in a pool of congealed and drying blood. An overturned chair lying nearby.

'Evening lads, we have to stop meeting like this,' Mac sighed.

'What have you got?'

'IC1 male. Shot twice in the chest. Also suffered a beating, see these two wounds on the top of his head? Not found the weapon yet. I need to take him back to the morgue and get him cleaned up so I can take a better look.'

'Was the attack in here or did it start elsewhere?' Monteith said.

'In here. There are no blood trails or splatters anywhere else in the house.'

'Do we have an ID?'

'The wife identified him. Adrian Knowles,' Mac confirmed.

'Where is she now?' Watson said.

'I believe she is next door with a neighbour. Family liaison officer is with her.'

Monteith turned to Watson. 'I think we may have a big problem.'

He was looking at some of the photographs dotted around the room. Adrian Knowles was pictured shaking hands with former Home Office ministers and local dignitaries. The photographs were from local and national meetings, some of which had large media coverage.

'Matthews is going to be in his element tomorrow,' Watson said, as he inspected one picture. 'If this is linked to the other two murders we will have trouble keeping it quiet. The media are going to have a field day.'

They spent the rest of the evening at the

neighbour's with Mrs Knowles. She confirmed that she and her neighbour had been shopping in the morning. Adrian had told her he was going to work in the garden. They came back around 2 p.m. and found him in the kitchen, dead.

No, they were not expecting visitors and no, he had not been threatened.

As they were leaving the house, the local media presence had grown. Uniforms were keeping them behind the tape at the end of the road. Even so, they were taking photographs of anything that moved and trying to interview anyone they saw.

A Police Constable approached Watson and Monteith at the bottom of the neighbour's driveway, introducing himself as PC Richard Parsons.

'I've spoken to all the neighbours along the road. Most were not at home this morning, but the owner of number 2 thought she may have seen something.' PC Parsons flicked through his notebook. 'She said she was looking out of the front bedroom window, when she saw a red car leaving the avenue at high speed at around 11 a.m.'

'Did she say if it was one of the neighbours' cars?' Watson asked.

'No. She said with it being a private road, she could recognise any of the neighbours' cars. And this was definitely not one – and she didn't see the registration number.'

CHAPTER SIXTEEN

Crompton and Lorimer, with two female PCs, were in Austin Lane to ask if anybody had seen Davis's RAV4 on the night he was murdered.

They split into pairs, Crompton and a PC covering one side of the lane, Lorimer and the other PC working the opposite side. The PCs were in plain clothes to avoid the sex workers disappearing in the shadows. Crompton wanted to be in and out as quickly as possible, depending on whether or not they got the information needed to crack Davis's murder.

They all agreed it would be better if the PCs talked to the women, showing each a CCTV picture of Davis's car. Crompton and Lorimer stood back, observing the area and noting the comings and goings. After the first hour they ended up with nothing. Either the women had not been in the area on that night, or they just didn't want to talk. Threatening them would be no use – it would just make them clam up and then say they were being harassed.

As they were taking a break, a woman's voice broke the silence.

'Little Kenny Crompton as I live and breathe. Looks like all of my Christmases and birthdays have arrived at once.'

Crompton turned round and came face-to-face with a mature lady.

'My God, Angie McDonald, you're not still in this business? What is it, twenty-five years?'

'Don't be cheeky, twenty tops.' She laughed, flicking her black, shoulder-length hair. Angie was dressed in a tight-fitting leopard skin top, showing all her curves. Knee-length leather skirt, calf-length boots and dripping with gold jewellery.

Lorimer and the PCs looked stunned and tried not to stare at Crompton and Angie's exchange.

'Don't worry I won't bite,' Angie said, tapping Lorimer on his cheek. They explained that they knew each other from Crompton's time on the beat, when he had helped Angie out of a few sticky situations. In return, Angie had kept her ear to the ground and passed on anything of interest. She was working the streets when Davis killed the two sex workers. Angie had known both women personally. Now she was more of a mother figure to new women, teaching them the dos and don'ts of the business.

'What brings you down here? In need of some company?' Angie teased.

'Jackson Davis.'

Crompton watched Angie shiver at the mere mention of his name.

'What's that bastard done now?' Angie said with distaste.

'He's dead. Murdered.'

Angie cheered, 'Good riddance.' Her cheer and smile disappeared fast when she clocked Crompton's stern look.

'Trouble is Angie, he was down here on the night he was murdered.' He showed her the CCTV picture of Davis's car. 'We came down to see if anyone remembers seeing it.'

'That's his car?' Angie said alarmed.

'Yes, why?'

'I did hear there was an incident with one of the younger women the other night, Cherry.'

A car pulled up across the road, a few yards down from where they were standing. A young woman got out, giving the driver the finger and a lot of verbal abuse.

'That's Cherry,' Angie pointed to the young woman. 'Looks like she had trouble with a punter. Do you need to speak to her now?'

Crompton nodded, 'Yes, I'm afraid so. If she has information, we will need to talk to her.'

Angie crossed over to speak to Cherry first. After five minutes of what looked like a heated discussion with lots of head shaking and arm waving, Angie beckoned them over.

Crompton said, 'Hi, Cherry, thanks for talking to us. We think you may have some information which could be helpful with one of our enquiries.' He showed Cherry the photo of Davis's car, 'Do you remember if you saw this car around over the last few nights?'

Cherry nodded, 'I was about to get in, but somebody shoved me out of the way.'

Crompton treaded carefully with his questioning, 'Do you remember what the person who shoved you looked like?'

She shook her head. 'He shoved me onto the ground, but I heard a lot of shouting from the car.'

'Shouting? Inside the car?' Crompton exchanged looks with Lorimer. 'Can you remember what was said, Cherry?'

'It was something like "drive now" and "what's good for you." Next, the car door shut and it took off, spraying me with muck.' She showed them the cuts and grazes she still had on her legs.

'Thank you Cherry. Would you be willing to come in to make a statement?' Lorimer said.

Cherry violently shook her head and backed off. Angie touched her arm lightly trying to calm her down. They stepped away for a moment and spoke in hushed voices.

'I'll bring her down tomorrow for a statement,' Angie said, coming back to them. 'She is young and naïve. She's also had a hard upbringing. Drugged up and drunk parents. Will the afternoon be alright?'

'Yes, thanks Angie.'

'Don't make it so long next time,' Angie whispered in his ear.

'I won't.'

CHAPTER SEVENTEEN

Susan walked into the house after another tough day at work.

Working there was hard. It was not the first place she would have chosen, but needs must. Family comes first, no matter what. She had to grow up fast after they murdered her mother. Her father had fallen apart before her eyes. Looking after him and trying to grow up as a normal child was hard. She had help from their next-door neighbours, Mr and Mrs Banks. Mrs Banks became more of a second mum to her. Susan had only been ten years old when her world had turned upside down. The Banks made sure she wanted for nothing.

As she entered the front room, her father was snoring, slumped in his chair. An empty bottle of whisky was lying on the carpet next to it. How long had he been there drinking himself into oblivion? What happened? She would get nothing out of him now.

Susan took a shower, trying to wash all the foulness of her place of work off herself. Drying herself in front of the full-length mirror, she stood and looked at her naked body. She still had all the curves in all the right places. At twenty years old, she should be out partying with friends and having fun with men. But she was stuck in a job she hated just to help her father out. She had been helping him for the last ten years, giving him all the love she had.

Because of that, she had missed doing all the things her school friends had done. Now they were going to university, taking a year out and going travelling, or getting married and having families. They had invited her to a couple of weddings, but she never went.

She did have a boyfriend in the last year of school His name was Shaun. But it only lasted a couple of months, nothing serious. Her father came first, and Shaun did not understand that.

She rubbed her body, looking at herself front and back. Cupping her small breasts, touching herself down between her legs wondering what it would feel like if a man did that. She lay down on the bed and brought herself to a frustrating orgasm.

She heard her father cough and splutter out of his alcoholic stupor. Sighing, she pulled on a pair of tracksuit bottoms, a T-shirt, and ran downstairs to check on him. He was still slumped in the chair but had finally come around. Staring out of glazed eyes, he was trying to focus on the surrounding room.

She left him getting his head right and went to start their evening meal. Putting on the DAB radio to the local station while getting things ready, she stopped dead when the news came on.

'Reports are coming in of a shooting in the village of Bennington.'

The newsreader, trying to add tension into his voice to emphasise the seriousness of the report, continued.

'The name of the victim has not been released, but we are led to believe he is a prominent local man.'

Susan did not need to be told who it was, she already knew. And it explained the state her father was in. She looked round to see him standing in the kitchen doorway. The eye contact between them was enough. No words were spoken.

Tonight was one for quiet reflection.

Watson arrived back home from Bennington late in the evening. The children were already in bed. Sally was busy at the kitchen table with school lesson planners, half a bottle of open wine by her side. She looked up and smiled as he came into the kitchen. So not to disturb her, he blasted his dinner in the microwave, took a can of John Smith's out of the fridge and retreated into his den.

After switching on his computer, he put Eric Clapton's *Slow Hand* CD in the stereo. Something calm to listen to after the day he'd had. A couple of mouthfuls of dinner and a long swig of beer, the computer was ready. The online local newspaper was already reporting on the shooting in Bennington.

Neighbours report that the dead man was Adrian Knowles, the former Governor at Claythorn Prison.

As he and Monteith were coming away, the television news vans were turning up, giving the local police a headache. But that was for tomorrow, Watson thought as he looked through the sports headlines.

He Googled Ronald Freeman's name. Pages of information popped up within seconds. Pictures, newspaper articles, and other documents including reports of the court case.

Since the internet became the so-called go-to place for information on whatever subject you are interested in, looking at historical and famous murder cases had become very easy. From Jack the Ripper to the Yorkshire Ripper. From Fred and Rosemary West to Steve Wright and the Suffolk Strangler.

The local newspapers had set up excellent internet sites, scaling back their daily paper versions. Most of what Watson was looking at was from the local Ravenswood Telegraph. Their lead reporter had done a superb job of recording everything – from the initial murder to the police investigation, to the court case and sentencing.

Watson took his time looking through some of the information until something caught his attention. 'Detective Investigated,' he read. He opened it and started reading. A smile turned into a broad grin as he continued. Watson opted to save the article in a folder, so he could look at it when he wasn't so tired.

Sally wandered in, glass of wine in hand. 'Tough day?'

'The worst and it will not get any better soon.' He showed her the headlines.

Sally put her wine down and started massaging his shoulders, easing out some of the tension. 'Just relax,' she told him.

'Relax? When you're digging your fingers in that hard,' Watson joked.

He took one of her hands and kissed it, swinging her around to face him. Moving her blouse up, he kissed her stomach. Sally played with his hair as he continued kissing her body.

Lay Down Sally came on the stereo. Sally stood back laughing. 'Good timing.' She took off her blouse and skirt, standing in just the briefest of bra and knickers.

'If you want to see more, you will have to come upstairs.' She slowly walked out of the door to the stairs, giving Watson an eyeful of her pert bottom with just a string of silk disappearing in-between her cheeks. Watson followed closely behind leaving Eric to sing to himself.

Monteith pulled into his driveway. Getting out of the car, he noticed a car cruising up the road. He stood as it drove closer.

'Nice set of new tyres you got there, pity to waste them,' the passenger said out of the window, laughing. The car sped off leaving Monteith cursing under his breath.

Katie opened the door in her dressing gown. 'Who was that?'

'Just some morons looking for trouble, no one to worry about.' Monteith moved past her, putting his keys on the hall table and taking his jacket off.

'After this morning, I'm scared,' Katie said with a worried look.

'There's no need to be.' Monteith took her head in his hands and kissed her on the forehead. 'I'm going for a shower.'

Monteith stood with the water flowing over him, shaking. He was scared too, and hadn't a clue how to get out of this mess.

CHAPTER EIGHTEEN

TUESDAY

The next morning, the CDA's office was likened to a scene from *DIY SOS*. New desks and new computers were being moved in to accommodate the influx of backroom staff Matthews had assigned to the agency.

Matthews had definitely gone overboard with things. The shooting of Adrian Knowles shifted things up a gear. No longer were the three shootings considered separate cases: they were dealing with a serial killer.

'So, tell me what we've got before I go in front of the mass media of baying dogs out there?' Matthews was glancing out of the window looking down at the ranks of television cameras and reporters milling around.

Crompton sat behind his desk. Frustrated in having Matthews in his office, preventing him from getting on with his day job. He had always hated the politics of it. Policing was catching the criminals whatever it takes. He updated Matthews with the visit to Austin Lane and Knowles's death, giving him at least something to feed to the press downstairs. Whether it satisfied Matthews, he could not care less.

With Matthews gone, Crompton called everyone into his office.

'I have just bullshitted the boss with a load of facts

so he can go and get mauled by the media out there. Officially we have a serial killer on the loose. That's not what we are telling the press, but that's what they will decide anyway. He will tell them something like, "Right now, we are exploring all avenues to catch the perpetrators of these heinous crimes."

The television in the corner of his office was turned on to *BBC News 24*, and it was projecting the live statement. The volume was turned down low.

Crompton needed to hear good news, 'So what have we got so far?'

Watson took his eyes off the screen. 'Ballistics said the same gun was used in both the Freeman and Davis shootings. A Glock .22, very common firearm nowadays. We've also got a partial fingerprint from the back of Davis's car, but nothing for a firm match from the database.'

'We have one of the sex workers from Austin Lane, who had a very lucky escape, coming in this afternoon to make a statement.' Crompton included his news in the round up.

'I hear you bumped into an old girlfriend last night, Boss?' Monteith said with a mischievous smile.

'If you are looking for me to bite back at that comment . . .' Crompton stared back at him. 'We believe now that Davis's assailant got into his car in Austin Lane and ordered him to drive away from there. Judging from the CCTV pictures Lorimer showed us yesterday, they went directly to the industrial estate. Hopefully, we can get a better description of the assailant later today.'

Crompton's mobile phone buzzed away on his desk. He picked it up, looked at it and diverted the call. 'What about Knowles?' he said.

'Mac is doing the autopsy today,' Watson said. 'Knowles was also shot, but he was hit over the head this time. Could be possible that whoever we are looking for is losing it. The first two killings were clinical, but this one was, I may be wrong, personal?'

Matthews had finished his media mauling, and the reporter was summing up.

'So who are we looking for?' Lorimer put the question out to everyone. 'A former prisoner with a huge grudge?'

'How many prisoners get released from Claythorn daily?' Monteith said. 'That's a lot of people to track down and interview.'

'Can we cut that down? When were Freeman and Davis released from Claythorn?' Watson put another question into the mix.

'I can't remember but I will go and look now.' Lorimer was already halfway out of Crompton's office to his desk.

Crompton's phone went off again. He picked it up, pressed a few keys and put it into his pocket. Getting out of the chair he said, 'Can you lot work this out between yourselves for now? I have a meeting I need to be at.' He picked up his coat and made his way out of the office saying nothing else.

'What do you make of that?' Watson nudged Monteith.

'He's probably going to see that bird down at Austin Lane,' Monteith replied as they made their way out of Crompton's office.

'I think there is something he is not telling us.'

'Are you still on about that? Just drop it and let's get on. Karl, have you found out about Freeman and Davis's release dates?'

'Both were released in the last six months, Freeman first.'

'When did Knowles retire as governor?' Watson said.

'If I remember rightly, one of those photos we saw

at his house was from a retirement party. I think it was about four months ago,' Monteith tried to recollect.

'I can just about get my head around somebody taking out Freeman and Davis, but the former governor of the prison, seriously?' Lorimer said. 'Whoever did that must have known we would be interested.'

Watson perched on the edge of a desk. 'It depends on the killer's state of mind. If he is determined it does not matter what we do. We might be dealing with a psychopath.'

Monteith thought of something else, 'How did the killer know when Freeman and Davis were released? Knowles is easy; they plastered his picture all over the local papers announcing his retirement, and the new governor coming in.'

'Good thinking,' Watson said. 'Was he released around the same time as them? We need to ask Claythorn for a list of inmates who were released then. Karl can you ring Claythorn and see if we can get that information? It'll be interesting to see what comes back.'

'I'll do it now.'

-X-

Crompton parked his car in front of the Dragon's Den. This was one visit he did not want to make, but he had to. He knew the reception he would get; it was just whether she would change her mind about seeing him at all.

He walked in through the front door and into the lounge side of the pub. The landlord, Peter Preston, was serving behind the bar. Crompton ordered a half of bitter then asked, 'Is Elizabeth around?'

'She is upstairs, who's after her?'

Crompton showed him his ID. 'It's regarding her brother.'

'I will see if she will come down, but after this

morning's press I doubt you will get the friendliest of conversations. And I'll warn you, she has been drinking.'

Crompton paid for his drink and sat down in one of the easy armchairs. He took out his phone and flicked through his messages. There was one from Watson, asking where he was and when he would be back.

'Look what the cat dragged in,' Elizabeth said furiously as she came into the lounge, full wineglass in hand.

'Hello to you too,' Crompton replied. 'You have a lovely way with words.' He waved his phone at Elizabeth. 'I had to look up some of the words you used.'

'Bastard.'

'Now I know the meaning of that one, and I am pretty sure I am not one of those. Can we go somewhere private?'

'Upstairs. The lunchtime crowd will be in soon,' Elizabeth barked, leaving Crompton in no doubt she was both pissed off and pissed.

She led Crompton through the kitchen and up a flight of stairs to the private flat above the pub.

As they entered the front room, Elizabeth turned to Crompton, arms folded. 'What do you want then?'

'It was you who called me, remember?'

'Oh yes, when were you going to tell me about this so-called, what did you say, serial killer? I saw it on the television this morning, just like that. No warning. Ronald's murder all out in public so everyone can . . .' her voice trailed off.

'We only worked it out this morning. It was my boss's idea to call the press conference. I had no say in the matter. I am sorry that you had to hear it that way, but I did not have the time to send anyone around beforehand.' Crompton tried to keep his voice calm.

'Bullshit. You never gave my family the time of day when Ronald was sent down. Why would you care now?'

'Your father. Because of Ronald's incarceration he threatened me and stopped me from seeing you.'

'You could have stopped Ronald from what he was going to do? Robbing that stupid newsagent's.'

Crompton stood firm, 'Yes, if I wanted my brains blown out. Nothing would stop him from committing that robbery. I had only just been promoted to detective. I tried to speak to him, but he said if I did anything to stop him, including grassing him up, both him and your father would make sure my time in the force would come to an end. If you get my drift!'

'I don't believe you. No, they wouldn't do that.' Elizabeth was incredulous.

'Believe me, they did,' Crompton confirmed as he sat in an armchair opposite Elizabeth, who was again nursing a large, full wine glass. 'Listen, I didn't come over here to drag over the past. I came to update you on what's going on.'

'Your boss beat you to that,' Elizabeth said with disdain.

Crompton took a deep breath. 'I also came to see if you or your husband had recalled anything from that night or even the days before. Sheila, over at your brother's flat, mentioned he told you both he thought he was being followed.'

'He was always saying things that made little sense. We took it he was struggling to take it all in after spending all that time in prison.' Elizabeth got up and refilled her glass.

'What things did he say?' Crompton stood next to her. He put a hand on her arm and spoke quietly. 'It might help in our investigation.'

Elizabeth took her time to reply. 'He said that he thought he was being followed.' Thinking again she said, 'Something about a red car hanging around.'

'Did he mention make or model?'

'No. After the amount of time he spent in prison the cars have changed a lot. I don't know what half the cars around now are called never mind him.'

'Where was this, did he say?'

'Outside the flat one time, then maybe when we were in town together. I don't remember.'

'When was this?' Crompton took out his notebook and started to write things down.

'I'm not sure. Sheila might be able to remember better than me.' Elizabeth sank back into her chair, tears in her eyes.

Crompton knelt down beside her. 'We will catch who did this, I promise. What you have told me today is a good start and it will help. We now have something else to follow up on. I will see about sending someone over to speak to Sheila again.'

'Thank you.' Elizabeth's voice was barely above a whisper.

CHAPTER NINETEEN

A taxi containing Angie and Cherry pulled up in the car park of the police headquarters. Cherry was dressed in a blue tracksuit and trainers whereas Angie was dressed as outrageously as the night before. Tight black leggings, a purple sequined top over a bra which enhanced her large breasts, leaving nothing to the imagination. A fake fur coat and sunglasses finished it off.

As they climbed the steps leading to the front door, two lads were coming out chatting. As soon as they saw Angie coming up towards them, they stopped and their jaws dropped. They were eager to hold the doors open, so they could ogle Angie more.

Angie smiled at them then down at the front of their jeans. 'Thank you lads. I think you need to do something about them.' She handed them her card. 'Call me.'

Inside Cherry started giggling. Angie just said, 'If you've got it, flaunt it.'

Cherry sat on one of the seats opposite the main desk while Angie approached the young officer at the desk.

'Angie McDonald here to see DCI Kenny Crompton.' The officer looked up from his computer, straight into her buxom bosom. The sight seemed to affect his voice.

'I'm, I'm sorry, who, who did you say you wanted to see?'

'That's a terrible stutter you have there. You should get that looked at.' Angie laughed at the officer's embarrassment. 'DCI Crompton; just say Angie McDonald is here.'

'Right, okay.' The officer tried to compose himself before phoning upstairs.

Angie sat back with Cherry.

The desk officer returned. 'DCI Crompton is out of the office at the moment, but TDS Lorimer will be down shortly.'

'Thank you, darling,' Angie replied.

'I don't want to do this,' Cherry suddenly said. Standing up, she ran for the front doors. Angie, quick as a flash, caught up with her.

'Don't worry. I will be in there with you.' Angie stroked Cherry's arm then held her hand, guiding her back to the seats. 'Listen, when I was your age the man whose car you were saved from getting into killed two sex workers. It scared those of us who were around at that time. Some so much they did not want to help the police because they thought if he found out they would be next. A couple of us thought differently and helped the police by keeping an eye out for him. Finally, they caught him. One of the women he killed was my best friend. This is why it's important for you to tell them what you saw, so we can get another killer off the streets.'

Cherry nodded and rested her head on Angie's shoulder.

Upstairs, Lorimer put the phone down after speaking to the desk officer. 'Angie McDonald, the woman the boss knew from last night is downstairs with our witness. When is the boss back?'

'I don't know, he has not returned my call or text,'

Watson said.

'Then I must see to it.' Monteith went to get out of his chair.

'Down boy,' Watson stopped him. 'This is our soon-to-be sergeant's interview. Karl, bring them up here. You can do the interview in one of our offices. The ones downstairs might put off our witness from saying anything. We need to keep her relaxed.'

Ten minutes later, they were in one of the side offices off the main CDA office. Cherry and Angie McDonald on one side of the table, Lorimer and PC Paula Dixon on the other. Drinks had been asked for and served.

Lorimer started. 'Thank you for coming forward Cherry. We value your help. The criminal justice system cannot work without witnesses. They are the most important element in bringing offenders to justice. We believe the information you have can help in finding the killer of the driver whose car you almost got into the other night. PC Dixon here will write down the conversation we have. You will then be able to read it over and make any changes that need to be made. First, I have to ask this. Are you willing to make a statement?'

Cherry looked at Angie for comfort, 'Yes I am.'

'I would like to take you back to last Wednesday night. Where were you and what were you there for?'

Cherry took a deep breath. 'I was on Austin Lane, working.'

'Can you tell us in your own words what happened that night?'

'I was standing waiting for another punter to turn up. A dark 4x4 pulled up next to me. The driver wound down the passenger window, and I went over to talk to him.'

Lorimer put several CCTV photographs of Davis's car on the table for Cherry to see.

'Could you please look at these?' Lorimer said.

Cherry picked the photos up one by one and studied them. 'This is the car that pulled up next to me. I recognise the man driving it.'

'Are you sure?' Lorimer pressed.

'Yes, you never forget the face of a punter or their car, especially the regular ones.'

'Was this man a regular? Had you seen the car before?'

Cherry hesitated looking at Angie, 'Yes he had been around a couple of times before.'

Lorimer glanced at PC Dixon who was taking the statement down. 'Have you got that?'

'Yes, Sir.'

'Now Cherry, can you tell us what happened next?' Lorimer was enjoying his first major investigation.

'As I said the passenger window was down. I walked over and leant on the door. I said something like, "fancy a good night."'

'So you spoke first?'

'Yes.'

'Did he say anything back?'

Cherry thought a moment. 'It was . . . "Get in and you will have the best night of your life." You never forget a chat-up line like that.'

'What happened next? Did you get in the car?'

'No, didn't get the chance.' Cherry took a gulp of her drink and looked at Angie.

'You're doing well.' Angie rubbed Cherry's arm.

'I went to open the door, but the next thing I knew I was pushed hard away from the car and fell onto the pavement. When I looked up someone else was getting into the back of the car.'

Lorimer realised the next few questions and answers would be critical to the investigation. 'Cherry, could you see who pushed you over before getting in the back of the car?'

'No, not from where I was, I just heard the shouting.'

'From inside the car?' Lorimer said.

'Yes. The one who got in the car was shouting, "Drive if you know what's good for you."'

'You're certain he said that?'

'Yes. He was banging on the back of the driver's seat shouting "drive". I got up and went to move out of the way, back to safety. I could see in the car before the door was shut.'

'Could you see the face of whoever it was in the back?'

'No, he was turned away from the door.'

'What about his clothes?'

'There was not much light, but I did see brown or tan shoes, dark trousers and a donkey jacket.'

'Are you sure about what he was wearing?'

'Yes. Again that is something we make sure we notice in case there is trouble with a punter.'

Angie was nodding as if to add credence to what Cherry was saying. 'It's one of the first things we teach the newcomers. Know your punters.'

Lorimer continued. 'What happened next?'

'The back door was slammed shut, and the car took off fast towards the city centre.'

'It there anything else you can remember?'

Cherry took another slurp of her drink. 'I don't think so.'

Lorimer looked at PC Dixon who was finishing writing the statement.

'Right I will leave you for a few minutes. You can go over what PC Dixon here has written and if you think of anything else, we can add that to the statement before you sign it.'

Lorimer left and headed straight to the coffee

machine.

'What's she said?' Monteith was keen to get all the details.

Lorimer walked over and sat down near to Watson and Monteith. 'Well, she's confirmed Davis was in Austin Lane that night and a man got into the back of the car and threatened Davis. She could not see his face, but has given us a description of his clothing. She is going over her statement now just in case she has missed anything.'

'At least we have firmed up some of the thoughts we had prior to her coming in and added a couple of others.' Watson went over to the information board looking at what they had.

Dixon stuck her head out of the door and called to Lorimer; he went back in and sat down.

'Right Cherry, you've read the statement. Is it correct?'

'Yes, there is nothing else I can remember to add to it.'

'If you remember anything else, please don't hesitate to get in touch with us. Here is my card, okay?'

Cherry nodded as she took the card. Angie gave Cherry's shoulder a rub and gave her an approving smile.

'I see you have already signed the statement and given your contact details. I think that's all for now. Thank you for coming in today,' Lorimer said, standing and shaking both Cherry's and Angie's hands.

'Tell Kenny I am sorry I missed him,' Angie said, when she left the room. 'Bye,' she added to Watson and Monteith before she and Cherry were escorted out of the office by PC Dixon.

'Bloody hell Karl, hope she behaved herself in there. Flaunting herself like that,' Monteith said when they were out of sight.

'She was the model of decorum while in there,' Lorimer said with a touch of upper class in his voice, which sent the office into hysterics.

'I trust you lot have got something of value to tell me, like we have caught the killer. Because if you have not why are we fooling around and not working?' Crompton had come in right at the end of the shenanigans.

'Sorry Boss,' Lorimer said as he went over to the board and updated it with what Cherry had said in the interview.

'You've just missed your friend Angie McDonald,' Watson said.

'No I haven't. I was accosted by her next to the lifts downstairs.' Crompton was still wiping the lipstick off his cheek as he came in and sat down at a desk. 'What did Cherry give us?'

'A lot less than Angie gave you it appears.' Monteith's remark sent the office into laughter again.

'Okay, okay, fun over. Point taken,' Crompton said. 'What did Cherry have to say?' He smiled.

Lorimer went back over the statement, giving emphasis to the new bits of information.

'So what have we got now?' Crompton said before running through the info on the board. 'The gun was the same one used for the Freeman and Davis shooting, and we are waiting for the autopsy on Knowles to find out if the murder weapon matches those. We have a witness giving us a partial identification of the killer from what she saw in Davis's car. And we have a possible sighting of a red car driving away from Knowles's house which did not belong there.'

Crompton thought. 'That woman who looks after the building where Freeman was living – didn't she say Freeman told her he was being followed?'

'Yes, but she and his sister put that down to paranoia,' Watson reminded him.

'I know, but it might help to clarify it. There was a

red car at Knowles's. There might be one at Freeman's flat? Watson, Monteith go and see her and check it out. Lorimer? Has the prison sent that list of released inmates through yet?'

Lorimer went over to his computer and searched his emails. 'It came in ten minutes ago. I'll make a start on it.'

Crompton went into his office, followed by Watson. 'Boss, I tried to get hold of you when Angie turned up.'

'I know, I got your messages.' Crompton was looking straight at Watson.

'I thought you wanted to be here for it, that's all.'

'I had important business to take care of. Lorimer sounded as if he was all right with the interview. Any problems I should be aware of?'

'No, no. We will get off now.' Watson left the office confused, thinking he had just missed something but could not put his finger on it.

CHAPTER TWENTY

Monteith pulled out into traffic and headed towards Thelwell. Watson was quiet in the passenger seat beside him. He put the car stereo on to break the silence.

'Old MacDonald had a farm, e-i-e-i-o,' Monteith started singing.

'What the hell are you listening to?' Watson finally said, still staring out of his window.

'Oh, you are still living.'

'Yes, but what the hell is that you have on?'

'Just one of Pixie's CDs. Thought we would have some music on!' Monteith said, straight faced, bursting into song again, 'With a quack-quack here and a quack-quack there.'

Watson reached over and turned it off.

'Okay grumpy, what's up?'

'I don't know. I still think there is something that Crompton is not telling us.'

'You still on about that?' Monteith shook his head. 'If he has something to tell that we need to know, he will. Now we need to get more information on these killings. Get over it.'

Just outside Thelwell they heard sirens. Monteith looked in his side mirror and spotted blue lights coming up fast from behind. They pulled over with the traffic and watched two Volvo squad cars and a Volvo dog handling car flash by.

'Looks like somebody called for some taxis to take them into town.' Watson grinned.

Monteith burst out laughing.

A couple of minutes later Monteith pulled up outside Freeman's old flat. They noticed that there were no lookouts outside the shop across the road, like the last visit.

'They must have gone to see which house the squad cars have been called to,' Watson commented, getting out.

They walked up to the door, knocked and when asked, showed their ID to the camera. Sheila opened the door and led them into her office. It had been tidied up, leaving them with more room to sit down.

'What can I do for you today, gentlemen? It's about Ronald Freeman again?'

'When we were here before you mentioned Ronald saying he was being followed. Can you help us on that? Did he say was it someone on foot or in a car?' said Watson.

Sheila sat back and thought. 'He mentioned nothing directly to me. It was something that Elizabeth commented on him saying.'

'How about the others that work here? Could he have said something to them?'

'It's possible. Do you want to talk to them?' Sheila picked up a radio. 'Mike, Steven, can you come to the office please?'

Both answered that they were on their way.

'Are you any closer to catching who did this?' Sheila said, 'I saw on the news you are looking for a serial killer.'

'Investigations are ongoing, which is why we are here,' Watson said.

'Plus, you don't always believe what the media says,' Monteith added. As he was saying it, his phone went off. Taking it out, he looked at the text message shaking his head. He replied and put it away.

As they were chatting, there was a knock on the door and Mike and Steven walked in. They were in their painting overalls and looked like they had more paint on themselves than on whatever it was they were painting. Following introductions they all settled down.

Watson started with the questions. 'Did either of you two speak to Ronald in the weeks leading up to his killing?'

Mike spoke first. 'Only in passing, really. He kept himself to himself. We took it to be a throwback from when he was in prison. He would say hello and mention if something needed checking in his flat, but nothing else.'

'Most of the time his sister, Elizabeth, was around with him,' Steven added.

'Did anything out of the ordinary happen during that time?'

'Like what?'

'Well, we are looking into the possibility he was being followed. His sister said he told her he thought he was being followed. Did you see anybody or any cars around the front of here?' Monteith said.

They looked at each other, and Mike finally spoke.

'He did come in after spending the evening over at his sister's. He was as usual a bit worse for drink, but he looked very agitated. I asked him if he was all right and he took me outside. He pointed across the road as a car parked there moved off. He said it had followed him back from the pub.'

'Did you get a good look at it?'

'At a guess, a red saloon. It was dark and with only the security lights from the front of here and the street lights to see by, it would be only a guess,' Mike said.

'Are you sure?' Watson pushed him.

'As sure as I can be.'

'Which way did it go when it left?'

'Back towards town. I ran down to the roadside when it moved off, but it was too far down the road to see anything else.' Mike shrugged his shoulders. 'That's all I can remember.'

'Did you see it again ?' Watson said.

'No we all kept an eye out for it, but I don't think it has been back.'

'Thanks for that lads, we will be in touch if we require anything else,' Watson said.

Later, as they were standing outside with Sheila, all the police cars they saw earlier went past back to the station. A fourth police van had joined the estate clear out while they were in the office. One kid who usually hung out outside the shop walked past.

'What's happened, Kevin?' Sheila said.

'The Claytons and Edwards were having their usual fight over territory. Six arrests I heard this time.'

'It should be entertaining back at headquarters tonight,' Monteith said.

'I would not want to be the custody sergeant when they get booked in,' Watson agreed as they got back into the car.

-X-

The trip back to headquarters was slow due to the rush hour traffic. Watson noticed that Monteith was getting fidgety and stressed. Shouting at other drivers and sounding his horn a few times. At one roundabout, a white van from a local courier company cut in front of them, causing Monteith to brake abruptly, followed by a volley of expletives at the driver through the open window.

'Calm down, Keith. Shouting won't get us there any faster, even though that driver is a moron for doing that,' he said, loosening his grip on his seat and door handle.

'I need to get back and away from work, that's all,' Monteith said sharply while looking at his watch.

'You on a promise from Katie?' Watson smiled.

'What? No. What you on about?'

Monteith's response was short and too quick for Watson's liking.

'Right, what the hell is wrong with you? What's getting at you so much that you are like a bear with a sore head?'

'Nothing is wrong with me,' Monteith bit back. 'If you don't want me to drive, you can always use your car. We always use my car.'

'Where the hell did that come from? Did I say anything about your driving or your car?'

Monteith pulled into the headquarters car park and parked up in the only space available, close to the rear entrance.

Watson changed his tactic using a more conciliatory approach. 'Keith, what is the matter?'

'Nothing's the matter, get off my back will you.'

Monteith jumped out and slammed his door, walking towards the rear entrance without waiting.

Watson got out, flabbergasted.

Monteith locked the car from where he was standing before disappearing inside.

When Watson went inside, the custody suite sounded like a mix of feeding time at the zoo and a barroom brawl. The custody sergeant was losing his voice with having to shout above the noise, and he was close to losing his temper as well. Nine officers were trying to keep order between the arrested Claytons and Edwards family members. They turned the air blue with threats from both families, and that was just from the women.

Watson headed for the door to go upstairs when he heard his name being called. 'Mr Watson.'

It was Joseph Clayton, the head of the Clayton family. He was waving his walking cane to make sure Watson knew who was calling him.

'Joe, what are you doing here?' Watson walked over. 'I thought there was a truce between you two?'

'Billy found out they were undercutting us on our merchandise and selling it on our part of the estate. He went over with his brother Davy to sort them out. I came down to try to smooth things over.'

'Sorting it out, meaning they went over to teach them a lesson.'

'You are putting words in my mouth Mr Watson. Now that is not allowed.' Mr Clayton wagged a finger at him.

'I've got work to do. Good to see you Joe.' Watson turned to leave.

'Your partner seemed a bit angry when he came in before you?'

'Case we're working on, nothing else.'

'Oh, okay. Pass on my regards,' Mr Clayton said with a smile.

CHAPTER TWENTY-ONE

WEDNESDAY MORNING

Susan sat at the kitchen table opposite her father.

It had been two days since he'd killed Adrian Knowles. This was the first time since then Littlewood was not either in a drunken stupor or nursing a massive hangover. Most of that time he had spent in bed, or in the bathroom being sick. When he hadn't reached it, Susan had to clear it up. It was not surprising since he had downed nearly a whole bottle of whisky on Monday.

Instead of leaving him on his own, she had rung in to work saying she had a migraine and would not be going in. It had been two years since he had been on a drinking bender. But confronting Knowles and killing him had sent him spiralling back. Susan searched and emptied the house of all other alcohol so her father could not be tempted again. She had to get control of her father and do it now.

She watched him tucking into a large fry up and a mug of tea. The first thing he had eaten in two days. Susan had tried to keep his fluids up with water while he was recovering, most of which ended up down the toilet.

She was not going to pry into what happened at Knowles's house because she already knew the outcome from the news. The television, radio and papers were full of it, and of the previous murders. Her father would tell her in his own time.

'That was good and hit just the spot,' Littlewood said, putting down his knife and fork after finishing his fry-up. He took a swig of tea and looked at Susan. 'How bad was I?'

'Very. Don't you remember anything?' Susan said after taking a mouthful of her tea.

'Nothing, not since leaving Knowles's house.' Littlewood's face was a blank.

It wasn't till after Susan filled him in on the missing two days he realised what killing Knowles had taken out of him. The others he could not give a damn about, but Knowles . . . He got up and came round to give her a hug.

'Thank you for looking after me. I don't know where I would be without you.'

'You would already be in jail, or buried with mum,' Susan blurted, slapping him angrily on the arm.

'Fair point, you've got me there.' Littlewood put his arms up in mock surrender. He picked up the newspaper and read the front page. 'At least the police don't have anything on us yet.'

'Yet being the operative word,' Susan reminded him. 'Getting caught now by making stupid mistakes is something we should avoid, especially after all the hard work we have put in.'

Susan pulled the little red book out of her dressing gown pocket. 'Fancy doing a bit of a spying?'

'On what, or should I say whom, do you have in mind?'

-X-

The smell of bacon and sausage baps wafted around the office along with strong percolated coffee. The officers from the CDA studied the list of recently released prisoners sent over from Claythorn. All two hundred and fifty-three of them.

'Welcome to the biggest game of Guess Who we have ever played,' Monteith joked.

'Boss, are we really sure that the killer is an ex-prisoner?' Watson said.

'No, but it's something we need to either confirm or pass over. We cannot do that without going through this list. Someone might stand out. What are you thinking?'

'Well, if you are doing this, with the former governor being murdered, do we include people working at the prison now or previously, when he was there?' Watson mused. 'Someone who is disgruntled?'

Monteith was getting frustrated. 'I thought we were trying to reduce the number of suspects not increase them. How many people even work at the prison?'

'We are trying to reduce it. Now can we get on,' Crompton said rhetorically.

'Why prison workers?' said Lorimer.

Watson explained his thinking, 'Because how does the killer know these people are ex-cons and are now out of prison? It has to be someone with the knowledge of the prison system.'

'Obviously!' Monteith grunted.

Watson ignored him. 'It could be an insider feeding information outside?'

'You and your theories. What proof have you got?' Crompton huffed.

'I just think we may be missing something if we only concentrate on released prisoners.'

'Let's do this first and if nothing jumps out at us then we will look at the workers, okay?'

CHAPTER TWENTY-TWO

Jimmy Russell stood surveying everything before him – his domain. Standing on the balcony overlooking the casino floor. His casino. Lying on the outskirts of the city, it played host to the local wealthy and would-be millionaires. Spending all their hard-earned cash. In his casino.

Russell came from humble beginnings. Born and raised on the Thelwell Estate, his parents were one of the first to move to the new council estate back in the 1970s. His entrepreneurial skills showed up early at secondary school by selling sweets in the playground, to the horror of the teachers. He got the cane. They found the snitch who grassed him up with a broken nose and a cut eye after Jimmy Russell and his brother Allan had caught him on the way home.

After leaving school at sixteen, he had joined his father and Allan in the car trade. Not the official car trade. The second-hand, ask-no-questions one where no one dared to complain or they would find out how dangerous and vicious the Russell's could be.

In his early twenties he could appear to be charming, but had a ruthless streak. If people said he couldn't do anything, he found a way. His way or a hospital visit. The end justified the means. He never married, but there were always rumours of children he was supposed to have fathered.

He bought up failing local companies and turned them around in his own way, putting his own people in to run them. If a disgruntled employee did not like his ways, they would find themselves seriously injured or worse. None of which could be traced back to Russell.

He became friends with councillors and the power brokers of the city. His first few millions came easily. If you were on the inside he rewarded you, but if you crossed him . . .

His older brother Allan came and stood beside him. 'Sometimes, Jimmy, even you outdo yourself. Getting the council to agree to the planning permission for this was a stroke of genius.'

'It helps, when you have something on the head of planning that he does not want to get out,' Jimmy smiled at his brother.

-X-

Susan brought the coffees across to where Littlewood sat in a well-known coffee establishment in the town centre. They were lucky to get a table near the front window as it was getting near to lunch time. It was already filling up with shoppers. Mothers with baby buggies blocking the way. Teenagers staring longingly into each other's eyes. Others with eyes locked on their iPhones. Office workers holding impromptu meetings in there because their work's coffee was cheap and nasty.

Across the pedestrian precinct was a shop being fitted out. One of the fitters was Duncan Healey, released from Claythorn five months ago after serving two years of a four-year sentence for helping run a cannabis factory in a residential area. Inside, he boasted how big he was working for a drug firm until someone bigger introduced him to the hospital wing.

'Interesting choice of subject,' Littlewood commented to Susan as she put sugar in her cappuccino.

'I thought you would approve,' Susan smiled back at him.

'Do you think you could do it?'

'Yes, I think it would be best if I took lead on this part of the project.'

'But you have done your fair share already. Is everything set with the other subjects?'

'Yes, the letters went out to the clients the other day. Nothing to worry about on that front.'

Littlewood looked across at the shop. 'Have you worked out how you are going to tackle the subject?'

'I thought we could work that out together,' Susan suggested.

Littlewood's face beamed. 'Sounds good to me.'

-X-

An hour after they had started they were closer to finding a suspect from the list of released prisoners.

'How many are we down to now?' Monteith was pacing the office trying to get his legs to work.

'Ten,' Lorimer called out.

'Anybody stand out?' Monteith said.

'All of them, depending on what you are looking for,' Lorimer replied. 'Robbery, ABH, GBH, murder, extortion, drugs. This is a list to die for. Don't excuse the pun.'

'Do any of them look good for our case?' Watson said, while pouring another mug of coffee.

'Three of them are a good possibility. Robby Davison: eleven years for murder, Ian Smith: four years for ABH, and Billy Clayton: five years for GBH with intent.

Watson turned, 'Billy Clayton! He was in the cells here last night.'

Crompton looked at his watch. 'They will be up at the court by now. You won't catch him there. Go and see what he says when he gets home. Before that, call in to see if Mac has done the autopsy on Adrian Knowles. Lorimer you can see what Davison has to say for himself.'

-X-

Watson and Monteith arrived at the morgue to find Mac's music blaring as normal. This time it was Johnny Cash's *Folsom Prison Blues*. Mac was stripping off his scrubs after finishing Knowles's autopsy. His body, covered by a sheet, was being put into the mortuary's cold chamber by Mac's assistant.

'Hello lads, come for your next instalment of Autopsy for Beginners?' Mac opened the bin and threw his scrubs in.

'No, just the findings please Mac. I don't think Keith's stomach could stand it,' Watson chuckled.

'It's all right I will stand back here,' Monteith was backing away to the other side of the room.

'This is not your normal music, Mac?' Watson commented.

'I am playing it out of respect for our visitor,' Mac said, as he opened the cold chamber and pulled Knowles's body back out. 'He was killed by two shots to the chest.' Mac pointed to the holes which were separated by the Y-shaped incision from the autopsy. 'But it's this which is the interesting thing.' He showed Watson the deep cut to Knowles's head just above the hairline at the front.

'Whoever did this was acting with force, maybe even anger. Looking at the deep lacerations here and here, his attacker hit him twice. Forensics found nothing at the house that looked like it had been used, so perhaps the assailant took it with him.'

Watson looked closely at the wound. 'Would the butt of a hand gun cause that much damage?'

Mac nodded. 'Maybe? And from the angle of the wound I would say you are looking for a left-handed attacker.'

Watson turned to speak to Monteith, but he wasn't there. He asked Mac's assistant if he had seen where he went, but he shook his head.

'Looks like your partner has done a runner again,' Mac exclaimed.

'Thank you Mac. Can you email me the report when you're done. I think I have a detective to catch– again.'

Watson strode out of the mortuary feeling frustrated with his partner. He stopped quickly, hearing a one-sided conversation.

'No, Mr Russell. I hear what you are saying. I will try but . . . Yes, 8 p.m. tonight, I'll be there. Thank you, Mr Russell. Goodbye.'

Watson walked around the corner as Monteith was trying to put his phone away.

'There you are. What happened? You were there one minute, then you disappeared.' Watson tried to sound concerned.

Monteith twisted. 'It's nothing. You know me and dead bodies in that place. I'm just feeling a bit queasy.

Watson patted him on his back. 'Just as long as you're all right. Let's go and see what Billy Clayton has to say for himself.'

CHAPTER TWENTY-THREE

The journey back into the Thelwell Estate was uneventful this time. At least Monteith put some suitable music on now: Meatloaf's *Bat Out of Hell.*

'Remember when we went to see him in concert?' Monteith turned the volume up.

'Yep, what an excellent night. Even with the other halves present,' Watson laughed. 'We need to arrange a night out again, just the four of us. Let our hair down. Old gits rule.'

'Don't say that last part in front of your Sally. She will ban you from the bedroom,' Monteith said, wagging a finger.

'Oh, and your Katie won't?'

'No, she will just ban me from the house,' Monteith laughed back, before both started singing along at the top of their voices.

As they got closer to the estate, Monteith turned the music down. 'You still think we are barking up the wrong tree?'

'Yes, I have a gut feeling we are.'

'Is that the same gut feeling you have about Crompton and the Freeman murder? Something he is not telling us?'

'Exactly the same. I think someone on the inside is feeding information out – when they're getting released, or have been released – and where to find them now.'

Monteith looked at Watson and shook his head. 'What are you suggesting? That they tell all the prisoners being released there is a psycho out there looking for ex-cons? I will tell you what will happen. Some of the hardened ones will say for them not to put anyone in their cell as they will be back for tea time after killing the bastard.'

Watson shrugged his shoulders as Monteith continued his rant.

'And half the people on the Thelwell Estate are ex-cons, or know someone who is. What do you want to do with them? Warn them? There will be vigilantes all over the estate gunning for trouble. It would make the feud between the Claytons and the Edwards look like a vicar's tea party.'

'That remains to be seen. Anyway, eyes on the road as we are here.'

Watson brought Monteith back to the matter at hand, as they reached the estate. Driving past the flats they had visited and the shop on the other side of the road, with the kids standing outside. They followed the road around and turned off into one of the side streets. The Claytons' place was half way down. A semi-detached house, with a large front garden and driveway.

As Monteith pulled up outside the Clayton house, the curtains began twitching in neighbouring houses.

'Neighbourhood watch,' Watson said, nudging Monteith as they walked up to the door.

Joseph Clayton had seen them pull up and was already opening the door.

'Mr Watson, Mr Monteith. What a pleasant surprise. Please come in. We don't stand on ceremony here.' Joseph stood, leaning on his walking cane. His frail body underlined his years, but his mind was still very sharp.

'You go and sit down Joseph, I have the door.' Watson watched as the old man slowly walked back to his chair near the fireplace.

'I see the neighbourhood watch is alive and well,' Monteith said as he was sitting down.

'Nosey buggers!' Joseph said back. 'Wish they would all bugger off.'

As they settled down with some small-talk, a red battered Vauxhall Vectra pulled up the drive. Watson and Monteith looked at each other. As the two men got out they looked and gestured towards Monteith's BMW.

'That will be Davy bringing Billy back from court,' Joseph said.

'You didn't go? Watson enquired.

'No, I've seen enough of the inside of the County Court to last me a lifetime. We are on first-name terms with the judges down there.'

The front door opened, and both men strode into the living room. 'Who the fuck has parked their car outside our house?' Davy shouted, before he realised his father had company.

'Lads, you remember DS Watson and DS Monteith?' Joseph hissed.

Davy apologised quickly. 'Oh sorry, didn't see you there.'

'That's all right. We are here to talk to Billy.' Watson was calm.

'What!' Billy exclaimed looking like he would lose his temper. 'I've just been to court and you want to fit me up for something else, no way.'

'Billy!' Joseph's voice was stern. 'Shut up and sit down. Mr Watson wants to ask you some questions about when you were in Claythorn.'

'Why? That was years ago.' Billy sat on the arm of his father's chair. Davy plonked himself in the spare armchair.

'You have heard about the ex-con murders recently? Well, you were in Claythorn at the same time as Freeman and Davis. Can you remember them?'

'You don't think I had anything to do with that!' Billy jumped up. 'I don't do guns, no, no way.'

'Calm down, we just want some information.' Monteith said.

'Billy,' Joseph shouted.

It was enough. Billy slowly sat back down.

'Billy, all we want to know is did you run into them while you were in there? Did they cause trouble while they were there?'

'Davis and Freeman? Davis not much, bit gobby; spent more time in the gym than anywhere else. Freeman was on my wing. Kept himself away from trouble, except for one time.'

'What happened?' Watson said.

'Don't know much, but he turned up one afternoon with a broken nose all taped up. Would not say what happened. The rumour was a prison officer had punched him after saying something he shouldn't have. Never found out the true story.'

'There's fighting in prisons all the time. What made this stand out?'

'Yes there was, but they were prisoners who wanted to cause trouble. Wanted to be the ones with the authority on the wings. Or those who were bored and took their frustration out by fighting. Didn't matter with who, other prisoners, screws . . . sorry– officers. Freeman was not like that.'

'Can you recall the officer's name?' Watson was taking notes.

Billy shook his head. 'No, not now. It was so long ago.'

'Billy, you realise I have to ask this as routine,

where were you last Tuesday and Wednesday night?'

'He was with me,' Joseph jumped in seeing Billy getting tense again. 'We were watching the European football on the television.'

'Who was playing?' Monteith said.

'Man United beat Copenhagen 3-0 on Tuesday, and Liverpool lost 3-2 at Inter Milan on Wednesday,' Billy said.

Watson looked at Monteith then the men. 'Well, thank you for your help. And, as always, if you remember anything else . . .'

Back in the car Monteith turned to Watson as he started the engine. 'Do you believe him?'

Watson shook his head, 'Not in a million years. He could easily have seen the scores on Sky Sport or the papers to cover himself. He might not be our murderer but he was doing something else those nights and not watching football.'

CHAPTER TWENTY-FOUR

Back at the office Watson and Monteith filled the others in on what Mac and Billy Clayton had told them.

'Well, my trip to see Robby Davison wasn't so fruitful,' Lorimer said. 'I met his ex-wife. She said they had split soon after he came out. He's now living somewhere in Spain. I've checked it out and he is, so we can cross him off our list.'

Crompton sighed, 'Okay, there's nothing else we can do. Get off home and we will look at it again in the morning. Watson, Monteith, can I see you in my office before you go?'

After tidying their desks and shutting their computers down, both wandered into Crompton's office.

'I have had word that Freeman's funeral is tomorrow. I want you two to go and keep an eye out. See if anyone turns up who takes an unnatural interest, or anyone who we know and have not thought of. You know the drill.'

'Babysitting a funeral?' Monteith was not happy. 'Surely we have better things to do.'

'Don't piss me off any more than you have done. You do what I ask you to, okay?' Crompton rattled back. 'It's at the cemetery at 10 a.m. and I want you both there.

Now get off home.'

Watson waited until Monteith had stormed out of the office, and then closed the door. 'Are you all right Boss?'

'What?' Crompton looked up from his paperwork. 'Yes, I'm okay.' He threw his pen down on the desk and leaned back in his chair. 'Matthews is on my back wanting a quick resolution to this horror show, and I cannot make him see we are doing all we can. Without a breakthrough, we're buggered.'

Crompton looked washed out. His normal demeanour had gone, and he looked like the weight of the world was on his shoulders.

'We will get the bastard,' Watson tried to sound upbeat. 'We have things to track. He will make a mistake and we will be there when it happens.'

Crompton looked at Watson. 'I wish I had your optimism because I don't see it.'

'Don't be too hard on Keith. He has things on his mind at the moment. I will keep an eye on him.'

Crompton did not seem to be listening as he had his eyes on his paperwork.

Watson left the office closing the door slowly.

'What's all that about?' Monteith said when Watson came out.

'He is getting grief from upstairs and is under the weather. Let's get out of here.'

-X-

Monteith dropped Watson off at his home. As he pulled away, Watson noticed Monteith didn't drive on towards his home but back into town. Quickly, he ran in the house to retrieve the car keys. Sally looked up from the television at him wondering what was happening.

'I will tell you later,' was all Watson could think of

saying.

'Grab a Chinese on the way back for us. Kids have eaten,' Sally shouted as he shut the front door.

He jumped into his car and tried to catch up with Monteith, hoping he could do so by the traffic lights. It did not matter if he didn't, Watson knew where he would end up.

Watson parked out of sight when he arrived at the casino. He managed to get there just in time to see Monteith go inside. He locked up and wandered inside, keeping his eyes peeled for his partner. The casino was not busy. People were playing on the fruit machines; some of the blackjack and poker tables had players. Two of the high-paying machines paid out their jackpot. Screaming and cheering came from the players and those around them. He saw one of them just sitting on the floor in front of the machine watching the money fall into the tray.

Watson sat at the bar and asked for a glass of lemonade, looking around for Monteith. After a few minutes he spotted him on the balcony at the far end. He was walking along with a couple of security guards or bouncers, Watson could not work out who they were as they disappeared through some large wooden doors.

Monteith was escorted into a large office. Sat at one end was Jimmy Russell, behind an ornate wooden desk. He was looking sternly at his computer while tapping at a few keys.

Monteith was roughly shoved down into a leather chair across from Russell.

'Gentlemen, that's no way to treat our guest.' Russell turned away from the computer. 'Apologise please.'

The two bouncers mumbled their apologies and stepped back, but remained within touching distance.

'Mr Monteith, glad you could join us. Would you

like a drink?' Russell was acting his imperious best.

'No thank you, I'm driving,' Monteith said nervously. He looked around the office, especially where the bouncers had taken up position.

'Oh don't leave me drinking alone.' Russell crossed to his drinks cabinet and poured a whisky and a glass of iced water. Putting the water in front of Monteith, Russell returned to his chair. 'I believe you have something for me?' Russell leaned forward.

Monteith fumbled in his jacket, pulling out a thick envelope, and lobbed it onto the desk. 'There's a grand in there. Would've been five hundred more but your goons slashed all four of my tyres.'

'Did they? Well, I am sorry if they got carried away. I will speak to them later.' Russell picked up the envelope and put it in his desk draw.

'You're not going to count it?' Monteith said.

'I trust you. But if you've short-changed me, well who knows what my boys could get up to after what happened to your car.'

'Have you finished?' Monteith felt he needed to get out of there before his mouth got him into more trouble.

'Yes, I think that concludes our business for tonight. I will deduct the money from the interest payments. You still owe me five grand,' Russell sneered at Monteith.

Monteith shot out of his chair towards Russell, but Russell's goons were faster, grabbing and holding him.

'Oh, by the way, on your way out take your lapdog with you.' Russell turned his computer screen around. On it was live CCTV footage. One was a close up of someone sitting at the bar. Watson.

Watson was looking round the casino floor when the whirlwind that was Monteith went past him.

'Outside now!' Monteith growled as he walked by.

Just as they stepped outside, Monteith swung

round and landed a right-handed punch to Watson's face which made him stagger back. Watson grabbed hold of his face and winced, not believing what his partner had just done.

'What the hell was that for?'

'Take your pick? Spying on me, letting Russell see you, not trusting me. Listening to my phone calls.' Monteith was enraged.

'Well if you had let me help with Russell and whatever trouble you are in, I would not have to.'

'It's none of your business!' Monteith stormed off, started his car and flew out of the car park, leaving the casino's clientele running and diving out of his way for safety.

CHAPTER TWENTY-FIVE

THURSDAY MORNING

The air was tense when Watson and Monteith arrived at the council cemetery just before the Freeman cortege. Following last night's altercation they arrived in their own cars, parking in the small car park at the front gates. Only official funeral cars and council vans were being allowed into the cemetery. Several cars were already there, so it was a tight squeeze to get into the last spaces available.

Having been told beforehand which plot Freeman's last resting place would be, they sorted out a good vantage point overlooking the area, not too close but close enough. Neither of them wanted to start a conversation. Egos took over. They mumbled good morning as they took their places.

Just along from where they stood, a middle-aged man was tending to a grave. They watched him clear the dead flowers and weeds way, putting fresh roses in their place. Kneeling down, he touched the headstone and looked like he was saying something.

Freeman's cortege pulled in through the gates. A hearse, with two official cars and three other cars following slowly made their way through to where the burial was to take place, parking close by. Elizabeth and her husband got out of the first car, with other family members alighting from theirs. Elizabeth looked around the cemetery.

Watson and Monteith were unsure if she had seen them.

Freeman's coffin was lifted from the hearse and carried by six pallbearers. The family following close behind.

'The amount of funerals I have seen over the years.' The man who was tending the grave nearby had moved next to Watson and Monteith. 'Some big and flamboyant, some small family only ones.'

'And this one?' Watson glanced at the man before focusing back to the funeral.

'Normal size. Looks like close family and friends. I take it you're not family?'

'No.' Monteith showed his ID card.

'Ah. Whose funeral are you interested in?'

'Ronald Freeman,' Monteith said, looking with frustration at the man who disturbed them.

'Oh, I read about him in the local paper. Nasty stuff. Is his murder one of the ones that this serial killer you're after did?'

'Investigations are still ongoing. Now, if you don't mind!' Monteith was getting pissed off with the interloper.

'I hope you catch him soon.' The man moved off towards the entrance.

'Stupid bugger,' Monteith mumbled under his breath. Watson looked at him and shook his head.

'What?' Monteith smirked.

Littlewood smiled to himself as he walked away from the two detectives. They stood out a mile. He knew whose funeral it was. He had spoken to the grave digger. It was just interesting to see the detectives here watching. What were they expecting to see or happen?

The killer turning up? That only happens in films, right?

When the man was out of earshot Watson tried to get Monteith to talk about the previous evening's events, but he was in no mood to reciprocate. Monteith was in big trouble and would not or could not accept it. It reminded Watson of when Monteith went through the same gambling addiction which almost broke his marriage.

Then it was the horses. Monteith could always be found in the bookie's when he was not on duty. And even when he was on duty, he wanted to know the results from that day.

Katie stood by him. They had only been married seven months, and she was pregnant with Rebecca. Monteith agreed to see Gamblers Anonymous and get counselling. It worked for a few years. But Watson could sense that this was much worse than back then. With Jimmy Russell on the scene Monteith's gambling had exploded. Nothing good came out of it. How had he got involved with Jimmy Russell? Why was Monteith behaving like this?

Watson could not let Monteith do this on his own. He needed to help his buddy, his partner, his long-time friend.

CHAPTER TWENTY-SIX

FRIDAY

For the last day and a half everybody felt they were getting nowhere. Banging their heads against a brick wall. No new leads were coming in but at least whoever this psycho was, thankfully, had not killed again. Watson stared at the information they had collected on the board for what seemed the thousandth time. He could hear a phone ringing. What had they missed?

Lorimer came and stood by him. 'Penny for them?'

'You'd need a pound coin for what's in here,' Watson joked.

'Only a pound?'

'I'll give you the first few for free.' Both of them tried to crack a smile but without success.

'The front desk has just rung. They have a Joseph Clayton wanting to speak to you.'

'Thanks, Karl.' Watson took the stairs down to the reception as the lifts were out of order again. That was three times in the last six months. At least he was getting exercise out of it. He did not even get through the door into reception before he was accosted.

'Mr Watson.'

Joseph was waving his cane around making sure he was noticed in the busy reception area. An elderly lady was reporting her bag being snatched. A man reported a builder's van for dangerous driving. Two homeless people, well known to the police, were sheltering from the heavy rain.

Watson sat down next to Joseph. 'What brings you down here in this bad weather?'

Joseph looked around the reception. 'Before I say anything, can we go somewhere out of the way?'

Watson agreed and went to look for an office not being used. One of the interview rooms was unoccupied, and he led Joseph into it.

'I hope you are not going to tape this conversation, Mr Watson?' Joseph said, sitting down.

'Only if you have something you want to confess to.' Both men laughed as Watson joined Joseph at the table.

'Now would I do a thing like that? No. First, I would like to apologise for abruptly ending your visit the other day. It wasn't good manners on my part.'

Watson waved the apology off. 'Don't worry about it. It's all water under the bridge.'

'Secondly, I asked Billy to really think about that altercation between Freeman and that prison officer, and try to remember his name. He said all he could remember was he had a name like Wood or Woods. They did not use first names unless you were chummy.'

'And it was definitely a prison officer that gave him the broken nose?'

'Billy said that was what he heard, but like we said before, rumours go around like wildfire. Most are not believed. But some end up being true.'

The rain was still coming down hard as Watson showed Joseph out before going back upstairs. He had asked Joseph if he needed a lift home, but he'd turned the offer down.

The reception was quiet; they had moved even the

homeless on. It was the smell, the duty officer told Watson. People were complaining.

Back in the deserted office Watson added what Joseph had told him onto the board and stood back. With it being a Friday and information seeming to have dried up, everybody had taken the chance to have an early start to the weekend. He had not noticed Crompton coming out of his office.

'You still here Terry? I thought you had gone?'

'I could say the same thing to you, Boss.'

'So what have we really got?' Crompton came over to the board. 'We are looking for a man who wears a donkey jacket, dark trousers and brown or tan shoes. He drives a red car, is left-handed and is possibly called Wood or Woods.'

'He also knows about the prison system and can handle a gun,' Watson added.

'Come on, let's get out of here, we can't do anything else tonight.'

'Is Matthews still giving you grief?'

'Why do you think I want to get out of here? He's still in his office and I don't want to get called up there at this time on a Friday. He thinks we should be here twenty-four/seven.'

They walked down the stairs together and out into the car park at the back of the headquarters, saying goodnight to the staff on duty and dodging the early weekend drunks being brought in by two vans. The rain had eased, but it was still drizzling.

'Talking of grief, you and Keith are treading on egg shells around each other. Had a lovers' tiff?' Crompton said, as he reached his car.

'He's got a lot on his mind and I overstepped the mark the other day thinking I could help. But he went in off the deep end.'

'Could I do anything? Talk to him privately?'

'I will leave that to you as he's not in your good books over the phone and Freeman's funeral. Like I said, I tried and failed.'

CHAPTER TWENTY-SEVEN

SATURDAY

Watson hoped the weekend would be relaxing, back to being a dad. Chasing a serial killer and trying to keep Monteith alive was more than one detective could handle. Three children and a wife sounded like a better deal, less dangerous.

Though not when you are asleep in bed, on your back, and your six-year-old daughter takes a flying leap on the bed and clobbers you in the privates.

Saturday morning was football morning with Simon. He played in midfield for Ryland under-fourteens and the team was doing very well in the league. Watson volunteered to run the line. Not because he wanted to, or it was his turn, but because he did not want to listen to the bickering from the side-line over the serial killer.

The other parents of Simon's team knew he had something to do with the police, as he knew what their occupations were, through general conversations before and after the matches. Nobody questioned him over the things he was working on, things in the newspapers or on local television. It was other spectators from either the opposing team or visitors who would talk about it. Most were okay, it was the theorists and police bashers he did not care for. He did not want to get into a slanging match putting them straight on the facts of the case. At least the linesman only got grief if he got an offside wrong. That he could handle with a big grin and some banter.

If his children kept him sane, his wife Sally kept him grounded. Fifteen years of marriage helped. He had seen the marriages of other police officers and detectives disintegrate before they realised things were wrong. Monteith's was almost one of those before it started, but they managed to pull themselves back from the brink. Yes, Watson and Sally had had rough patches, all marriages do.

After the football came the gardening. Tidying up the flower beds and cutting the grass. Rachel was doing her best to help. Dressed in her red coat and red wellies, she was putting the weeds into her bucket, carrying them to the compost heap at the bottom of the garden. Both of them were dodging the flying football from Simon and Jason. Simon was teaching Jason some tricks and skills he had learnt during training.

It was different over at the Monteiths' home. Life at the moment was akin to a battlefield. He had not spoken to Katie for days, choosing to keep himself to himself, keeping thoughts of the mess he had got himself into in his head.

He usually got home late. Rebecca and Pixie were always asleep. Katie was sometimes up waiting, but most nights she was asleep as well. When she was up, it usually ended in an argument.

When they did talk, it was a one-way conversation as Monteith could not bring himself to tell Katie the full story of the deep cavernous hole he was in. He knew he should because it affected his whole family.

Their savings had been depleted, meaning the holiday they had booked to Spain might as well be cancelled. He didn't even know if he'd be around, especially after Jimmy Russell had finished with him.

Where was he going to get five grand? It would have been four grand, but for Russell taking the grand he had given as interest payment instead.

CHAPTER TWENTY-EIGHT

SUNDAY MORNING

Duncan Healey was never one of the big men while he was in Claythorn. He was just a small cog in the big machine that is the drug industry. It was his attitude while he was inside that bugged not only the prison officers but also other prisoners. He had only been taken on to look after a cannabis factory in a rented house, and he could not even get that right. Caught in the act after coming out of the house one evening completely stoned as a police car was driving past. In prison, he acted like he was Mr Big, that's until they introduced him to the real Mr Big in the drug world. Two weeks on the hospital ward followed, after he was found at the bottom of the wing stairs with a broken leg and a broken arm.

Now working for a shop fitter, he was trying to turn his life around. He had even started jogging through the parks and around the lakes of West Ravenswood. He had gone out early this morning on a route, taking in the river and, with few runners out this early he felt as if he was on his own, just him and his music on his iPod. So it was a surprise when he approached the bridge over the weir, to find another runner. She was lying down, holding her ankle and crying.

Duncan ran over, switched off his music, and knelt

down. 'Can I help you?'

The runner tried to answer through her tears. 'My ankle, I went over on it coming off the weir.'

'May I take a look?' Duncan smiled, trying to put her at ease.

'Yes, but be careful.'

'My name's Duncan.' He straightened her leg so he could look at the ankle properly.

'Susan, and thank you for helping. I don't know what I would do if you hadn't come along.'

'Does this hurt?' Duncan moved her foot slowly. Susan winced. 'On the outside of the ankle.'

'There does not seem to be any swelling yet, but the sooner you get ice on it the better. Do you think you can stand on it?'

'I will try. I parked my car the other side of the weir.'

'You can't drive with that ankle.' Duncan helped Susan up, letting her put her arm over his shoulder for balance.

'I'm not going to drive. I will phone my father, he can come and pick me up.'

They walked back over the weir at a gentle pace. Duncan's mind was racing. Coming to the aid of a beautiful woman dressed in black, knee-length Lycra shorts and a tight, yellow top under a blue tracksuit, all his birthdays had come at once. He noticed she was not wearing a ring on her finger either. They were halfway across when he noticed a man coming towards them.

'What are you doing with my daughter?' The man shouted.

A shocked Duncan switched his gaze between the man and Susan.

'Dad, what are you doing here?' Susan shouted back.

'I said what are you doing with my daughter you

piece of shit?' He roared, dashing towards them.

'Dad, he is helping me. I hurt my ankle.'

'Shut up. I was talking to this piece of crap.' Littlewood pushed Duncan away from Susan and pulled out his gun.

'Whoa . . . take it easy. I was only helping your daughter with her ankle. Tell him Susan.' Duncan was up against the bridge edge with a gun at his chest.

Susan stood there with a big smile on her face waving at him. She had played her part brilliantly. 'It's better now Duncan, thank you.'

'What's this . . .?' Duncan was struggling to get his head around what was going on.

'Message for your drug friends, drugs kill,' Littlewood said with vitriolic passion. Glancing around him to check no one was nearby he stood back and fired two bullets into the chest of his victim.

Duncan's eyes glazed over as he fell into a crumpled heap.

Littlewood grabbed Duncan under his arms and Susan took hold of his legs. They struggled to get his body over the bridge edge and into the weir, but managed to topple him over, and watched him disappear under the fast-flowing water sweeping under the weir.

Littlewood hugged Susan and started back to their car. 'How's your ankle?'

'Race you to the car and you will find out,' she said taking off, leaving Littlewood laughing.

CHAPTER TWENTY–NINE

MONDAY

Crompton arrived early in the office, trying to catch up on paperwork before being hit by the force that was Matthews. Normally the big bosses were nowhere to be seen, dealing with overseeing strategy and police standards, along with finance. Schmoozing with local bigwigs and dignitaries and attending high grade meetings concerned with making the police better.

That is until things like serial killers are on the loose, and the bosses come running to get their faces on the television and in the newspapers. Then you cannot get rid of them.

Crompton's first task were his emails. All one hundred and thirty-seven of them. Most of them had come in over the weekend. Nine of them from Matthews wanting this and that. The deletion button came in handy at this time of the morning, especially before Crompton had had two cups of strong coffee.

One email caught his attention. It was from a newspaper and titled, Would you like to comment on this?

Attached to it was a Media Player film clip. He clicked on it. A piece of CCTV security footage greeted him. Crompton looked closely and his anger rose as the clip continued and he saw what was developing before him. By the end of the video his blood had boiled. He emailed a reply asking where they'd got the clip from, not expecting an answer.

Watson arrived just as Crompton had watched the clip for the third time, trying to get his head around what he saw. He called Watson into his office and showed him the clip.

'Did the sender say where they'd got this from?' Watson said, knowing the answer already.

'I am waiting for an response, but you know what the papers are like for a story. What the hell was it about?'

'I think it's better coming from him than me,' Watson said. 'If he found out I have been talking, you might find one of us in A&E.'

Crompton called both of them in later that morning. He had turned his computer screen around so both could see, waiting until they'd both sat down. Watson was trying to look relaxed.

'A newspaper reporter has sent me a CCTV clip from a couple of nights ago and has asked me to comment on it before it goes public. I wanted you to look at it before I do that,' he said, pressing *play*.

It showed Monteith arriving at the casino and going inside, being met by a pair of suited and booted security guards. They disappeared upstairs and through a pair of big wooden doors. The CCTV then switched to Watson sitting at the bar drinking and looking around. Next was Monteith striding towards Watson and both leaving the casino. The last shot was of Monteith punching Watson, them arguing and Monteith speeding off.

When the clip finished Crompton sat back and waited for someone to say something, eyes fixed on them. Waiting for them to explain, and fast.

Watson sat still looking back at his boss, but he could tell that Monteith was about to blow.

Crompton broke the silence. 'Well?'

'It's none of your business,' Monteith shouted. He stood up and reached for the door.

'DS Monteith, if you set foot out of this office without explaining yourself I will suspend you straight away and Matthews will have to get involved. Now get back here and sit down. Whatever the problem is, it will not go away if you behave like a spoilt brat who has got his fingers caught in the till.'

Monteith hesitated, fight or flight. Flight and he gets suspended. Fight and he accepts the consequences. He slowly turned back and sat down.

For the next hour Monteith spilled everything regarding Jimmy Russell, knowing he could not continue like this. He needed help and fast.

He started going to the casino with some mates about six months ago. It started out as a bit of fun, playing on the slot machines and having a few games of blackjack. During these visits he slowly lost control, betting more.

His friends tried to curtail him but soon realised they were out of their depth, and they soon stopped going to the casino with him.

Monteith said he had met Jimmy Russell there one night when he was on his own. They started talking and the upshot was he was introduced into the big league. Starting with invite-only small stakes poker which took place in the rooms at the back of the casino. Monteith said he did well during those games, winning more than losing.

By that time his gambling habit was at its height. Winning was becoming the normal, coming away some nights with up to three grand up. Then Russell let him sit in on some of the high-stake games. That's when it started to go wrong.

In the end, he owed Russell five grand. Russell

banned him from the tables until the debt was paid. To add to the incentive, Russell sent his goons round to slash the tyres of his BMW.

'The night those CCTV pictures were taken, I had gone to pay off a grand of the debt. Russell said he would take it as an interest payment and I still owed the five grand. I did not know Watson had followed me, which is why I reacted the way you saw.' When Monteith finished, he looked drained.

'So we can take it Russell leaked the CCTV pictures to the paper,' Watson said. 'To show us that he can do what he wants.'

Crompton sat contemplating what he had just been told. He could rant and rave about how stupid Monteith had been, but what good would that do? Send him home and lose a good detective in the middle of a major crime? Monteith had probably been through the wringer both at home and with Watson but he must have known what he was getting himself into when he started gambling again.

'When does Russell want the five grand you owe him?' Crompton said.

Monteith looked beaten. 'You know Russell, he always wants things straight away or else.'

'I will have to tell Matthews about this, especially as the papers have got hold of it.'

'I'm dead anyway, what's another knife in my back going to do.'

Lorimer was updating the information board when they walked out of Crompton's office. Lorimer had added three names, Gerrard Wood, Peter Woods and Colin Littlewood.

'I've just got off the phone to Claythorn,' Lorimer said. 'I was following up on what Clayton said about Freeman's altercation with the prison officer. They could not confirm that the incident took place because there are so many fights and beatings in there. Like all prisons, it's difficult to track down one from that long ago. But they gave me the names of three officers who were around at that time with Wood in their surname. All were working there when Freeman, Davis and Knowles were there. Claythorn are sending over what they have on record for all three.'

'This will not be another wild goose chase?' Monteith tried to get involved but was still subdued after the grilling he had just been given.

'Sorry, but not all killers hand themselves in to police, some we have to catch,' Watson said sarcastically, looking over at Monteith.

'Ha-bloody-ha.' Monteith stormed out of the office, leaving everyone else staring at each other.

'Who upset him?' Lorimer said.

'Family troubles, nothing to worry about.' Crompton said. 'Right, when we get the info from Claythorn we need to track these three down and see what they have to say.'

Lorimer went back to his desk, 'That's just come in. It includes last known addresses.'

'Watson, find Monteith, wherever he has gone and you two can go and interview Colin Littlewood. Lorimer, you and I will visit Peter Woods. Whoever finishes first gets Gerrard Wood as a bonus.'

Monteith was outside pacing around the car park cursing to himself. Looking up, he saw Watson coming out of the door.

'I'm finished, you know that. Screwed. If he tells Matthews about this I am out of here. You know what a straight-down-the-line, by-the-book officer he is.' Monteith slammed his fist down on the roof of his BMW, leaving a slight dent in the metalwork. 'Bollocks.'

'They won't get rid of you. They need you too much.' Watson tried to play it down.

'Oh yes, says who? Lorimer is gunning for his

promotion. Why not get rid of the embarrassment and promote Lorimer?'

'You forget I was in that CCTV, they get rid of you they will also have to let me go.'

'No, they won't.' Monteith was shouting at Watson, causing the other users of the car park to turn and look. 'You will just go down to desk duty for the uniforms.'

'Why don't you listen to yourself. You're not the first officer to have a gambling problem and you're not going to be the last.'

'Yes, but I bet none of them owe it to the biggest lunatic in the city. If Matthews doesn't get me, Russell will. I cannot pay him off; like I said, I'm screwed.'

'Calm down, we have to go and visit one of the prison officers, Colin Littlewood, and see what cock and bull story he has to tell us.'

CHAPTER THIRTY

They took the long route to Littlewood's house so Monteith could calm down. The silence in the car was deafening.

After parking on the street they walked up the drive past a white Renault Clio and knocked on Littlewood's front door. There was no answer so Watson knocked again while Monteith looked through the front window into the living room.

'They have gone on holiday.' The woman from next door was standing on her doorstep.

'Do you know where, Mrs . . .?' Watson said, as he approached her, showing her his ID. Monteith followed with his ID out. The woman looked closely at them before she replied.

'Mrs Banks. And no, I don't know where they went. We came down for breakfast this morning and there was a note through the door from Colin saying they had gone away for a few days.'

'Do they often go away like this?' Monteith said, putting his ID back in his pocket.

'No. I cannot remember the last time they went away for a holiday or even a weekend. Why do you want to know?'

'We need to talk to Mr Littlewood regarding an investigation. Have you known the family long?'

'Ever since they moved here, twenty-odd years ago. Very nice family. Oh, here's my husband.'

As they were talking, Mr Banks walked up the drive towards them with his dog. Both Watson and Monteith showed him their IDs.

'Morning, officers,' Banks said.

'They're asking about Colin.' Mrs Banks updated her husband on the conversation.

'Well, don't stand on the doorstep, come in.' Banks ushered the detectives past his wife, who gave him a look of disgust.

They all went into the living room and sat down. Monteith and Watson on the sofa, Banks in his chair, with Mrs Banks hovering around.

'So you want to know about Colin?' Mr Banks said.

'Your wife said you have known him for about twenty years?' Monteith said.

'Yes. Colin and his wife Jackie moved in next door about then. Very nice couple. She was pregnant with their daughter Susan at the time.'

'And when they moved in, where was he working? Did he have a job?'

'If I remember, he had just started working at Claythorn Prison.' It suddenly dawned on Banks why they were looking for Colin Littlewood.

'You don't think he is involved in all these killings are you? No way, not Colin. He's not been in a fit state to do anything over the last few years. Not since his wife was murdered a decade ago.'

Watson and Monteith looked at each other. This was new information.

'What happened with his wife?' Watson said.

'You don't know? She was pushed down the stairs at home by two burglars when she confronted them. He was at work when it happened. Jackie died in hospital. After that he went to pieces, depression and alcoholism. Lost his job at the prison. My wife looked after Susan as she was growing up because he couldn't. If you think he is involved in all these killings, you are wrong. He hardly goes out. The only time he does is with Susan, or to the cemetery to put flowers on Jackie's grave.'

Banks was getting furious. 'I tell you something. When he heard about that governor of the prison being murdered he was so upset over it, Susan told me he drunk himself into a stupor, not wanting to believe it. Is that someone who could murder someone? Tell me?'

Mrs Banks came over to calm her husband. 'Asthma,' she said, as a coughing fit took over his body. She gave him his Ventolin inhaler.

Watson and Monteith talked quietly letting Banks catch his breath before continuing.

'Mr Banks, are you okay to continue? We only have one more question to ask,' Monteith said.

Banks nodded.

'You said he lost his job at the prison after his wife died, do you remember why?'

Mr Banks leant back in his chair bolstered by cushions. 'Something about a prisoner goading him over losing Jackie, Colin snapped and hit him. That was enough for the prison to get rid of him. He was not well at that time. Losing Jackie hit him very hard and he couldn't cope with the grief and he took to the bottle. We brought Susan up more than he did during that time. Helped her with her homework, took her in to sleep over when he could not look after himself never mind Susan. Saw her turn from a girl to a young lady then woman. Social Services got involved and wanted to put Susan into care, but because we said we could help out she stayed, thank God. Losing Susan would have just finished him.'

They thanked the couple for their help, and Mrs

Banks showed them to the door.

Monteith quickly said, 'Mrs Banks, just to confirm, Mrs Littlewood is buried in the cemetery?'

'Yes, why?'

'Oh nothing, I can't remember if I made a note of it when your husband was talking. Thank you.'

Walking back to the car Watson said what they were both thinking. 'We've met Colin Littlewood already.'

They rushed to the cemetery and to the place where they were stood for Freeman's burial.

'Where was he?' Monteith began looking at headstones.

'Over there I think.' Watson shouted as he ran from headstone to headstone.

'I've found it, over here,' Monteith called out. 'Jackie Littlewood's headstone.'

Watson weaved through the lines of graves to where Monteith was standing. 'It was him. We spoke to him,' Watson said in a frustrated tone.

'He knew why we were here; he knew Freeman was being buried that day. The bastard.' Monteith was going spare.

Watson read the inscription on Jackie Littlewood's headstone.

Her Life A Beautiful Memory
Her Absence A Silent Grief

'This is more like un-silent grief,' Watson murmured.

CHAPTER THIRTY-ONE

Dumping her dad's Škoda and hiring a 4x4 in her mother's maiden name before taking off was a great idea of her father's.

They left it in a supermarket car park, unlocked and with keys in the driver's footwell, while getting supplies. It would soon be spotted, but they would be long gone before that happened. An hour later they pulled into the woodland holiday park.

Susan had booked a log cabin deep in the woods for a week. They would not be staying for that long, just a couple of days. The next stage needed to be planned thoroughly and set out. If they had stayed at home, their nosy neighbours might disturb them.

Mr and Mrs Banks were a lovely couple, and both her and her father were indebted to them. After her mother was murdered, they'd helped bring Susan up, but sometimes they were a pain. Spending time away would prevent tongues wagging. Here, there was no one to bother them.

Susan and her father unpacked and stood on the sundeck with a soft drink taking in the surrounding scenery. They had chosen the most secluded cabin on the holiday park so none of the other holidaymakers could see them.

The local ducks were wandering around as if they owned the place, organising themselves into raiding parties knowing that they could be fed nicely by visitors. Susan spotted a couple of squirrels scurrying up and down a tree, playing and looking for food. She pointed them out to her father who smiled and had a little chuckle. Something he had not done for a long time. The surrounding trees were full of birds chirping and squawking, seeing who could be the loudest.

Littlewood sat back on one of the wooden chairs on the decking and closed his eyes, taking in the sun.

Susan, sipping her drink, leant against the fence that surrounded the decking, looked at him and smiled. The contentment on his face was a joy to see.

CHAPTER THIRTY TWO

'You are sure we've got this correct?' Matthews said as Watson stuck the pictures of Colin Littlewood and his daughter Susan on the information board.

'Yes, we are positive Colin Littlewood killed Freeman, Davis and Knowles,' Watson replied. 'He killed Freeman because he had a run-in with him in HMP Claythorn. Littlewood bust his nose because of what he said about his wife, Jackie's, death. Also, because of what Freeman was in prison for. He turned up at Freeman's funeral; we even spoke to him, not knowing what we know now. Knowles, because he was Littlewood's boss. He sacked him after all he had been through. And Davis, for what he had been in prison for. It could have been for shooting his mouth off while he was in there. Littlewood might have wanted to get revenge for what he had to put up with while he was working there, a vigilante killing.'

'Pity we can't let him continue.' Monteith let out a sigh.

'Only you could say something like that,' Crompton said, shaking his head. He caught Matthews doing the same.

'I know, bad taste,' Monteith said. 'But it's what most of the public think. Prison is too good for some of these creeps And Davis was the biggest one around here.'

'Do we know who killed Littlewood's wife and are they still inside?' Matthews said.

'I contacted Claythorn an hour ago, but they have not got back to us as yet,' Lorimer chipped in.

'Press them for an answer now, it's imperative we know– for their safety,' Crompton said. 'We need to find them and either warn or protect them.'

Lorimer's phone rang. 'Yes . . . Where? Are you sure it's his? Thank you, can you hang on?' He turned to the others. 'That was the control room. They have stopped Littlewood's car for speeding in the town centre. Asked what you want them to do next?'

'Hold them and we will be there ASAP.' Watson and Monteith grabbed their jackets and ran towards the door. 'Text us the position will you?' Monteith shouted back.

Within ten minutes they had pulled up behind the squad car and Littlewood's car. Walking rubberneckers stopped as if this was the first time they had seen someone pulled over by the police.

Watson and Monteith looked at each other as they approached the cars. Something wasn't right. 'They're still in the car,' one of the uniformed officers said. 'He has failed a breath test and there is a strong smell of cannabis.'

Watson knocked on the driver's side window. It was wound down, the driver was not Littlewood. In the seat was a thin, haggard-looking man, stinking of alcohol and cannabis. Beside him a young woman who also looked as if drugs and drink ruled her life.

'Can I help you, officer?' the man slurred.

'Is this your car?' Watson said, pissed off that it was not Littlewood, and knowing full well what the answer was.

'Yes, it's my car. We have just been shopping. I told the officer that.' The driver replied matter-of-factly.

There were Tesco shopping bags on the back seat. Cans of beer had spilt out and a bottle of vodka could clearly be seen through one bag.

'Can I see your driving licence, please?'

'Erm. I must have left it at home. I can bring it around later?'

Watson had had enough. He told the officers to arrest them and they would be dealt with back at the station.

-X-

Lorimer printed off the information he had just received from Claythorn prison, re-read it and headed to Crompton's office. After Watson and Monteith shot off to apprehend Littlewood, Crompton and Matthews had been shut in Crompton's office deep in conversation.

Crompton waved Lorimer in as he closed a file on his computer.

'I've just heard from the prison. Littlewood's wife's killers Andrew McNulty and Thomas Smith are still in there. But they are due to be released soon,' Lorimer said, as he came to stand by Crompton's desk.

'Did they say when that would be?' Matthews said.

'No. They refused to give that info to a mere junior like me. Something about data protection?'

'Typical. Give me the phone number. I'll rattle their cage.' Lorimer handed the paper with the information to Crompton. 'Any news from the daring duo?'

'It was Littlewood's car, but it was stolen from a supermarket by a couple of druggies. Uniform are bringing them in now.' After a couple of nods and thank yous, Lorimer shut the door.

Crompton opened the bottom draw of his desk, and brought out a bottle of whisky and two glasses.

'Bit early, Kenneth, for this?' Matthews raised his

bushy eyebrows.

'Only medicinal. After the day we've had . . .' Crompton pushed a glass across the table. Matthews took it, swirled the whisky around and took a sip. 'Yes I agree, just medicinal.'

'So what are we going to do with Monteith?' Crompton eased his chair back and came round his desk, sitting next to Matthews.

'Besides shooting him for being a moron.'

'Well I hadn't thought of that, but I suppose that could be arranged.'

'Joking aside,' Matthews said, swirling his drink around inside the glass, 'I will deal with the editor of the newspaper. When he's made aware that certain doors will be closed if they run this casino story, I think he will change his mind. As for Monteith . . .' he looked at the contents of his glass . . . 'could we use him to get Jimmy Russell?'

What his boss suggested surprised Crompton. 'You want to use Monteith as bait, go undercover? Grant, I didn't think you could be so devious.'

'No, not so much undercover. He already knows Russell. But what if he could get closer, see what else he is planning?'

Crompton wasn't so sure. 'I don't know if he's that close to Russell, he owes him money, but he is not friendly with him.'

'Maybe it's time for him to get to know him better?' Matthews would not let this chance to bring down Jimmy Russell go.

'And the five grand he owes?' Crompton said.

'We will give it to him to soften the deal. Say it was operational expenses to the finance department.'

Crompton got up, going back behind his desk. 'Do you honestly believe he will go for it? I don't.'

'Don't give him a choice, if he wants to continue as

a detective.'

'You can't be serious, Grant?'

Matthews looked at Crompton with a knowing smile as he got up. 'Well if that's all, I have to sort some things out upstairs. By the way, that whisky is very good; we must be paying you too much if you can afford that.'

Matthews was leaving Crompton's office as Watson and Monteith arrived.

'He's done a runner. The bastard's done a runner.' Watson threw his jacket down. 'Littlewood's dumped his car and is laughing at us because we can't catch him,' Watson said.

Matthews stopped. 'Anything caught on the CCTV at the supermarket?'

'No, that's where we have just been. You can see Littlewood park up his car and go into the supermarket, but we lose him in the crowd. Don't know where he went after coming out. If he got into another vehicle waiting for him, we didn't see him.' Watson was grabbing a drink and something to eat as he filled Matthews in.

Monteith continued, slumped in his chair. 'His daughter's car was still on the driveway when we interviewed their neighbours, Mr and Mrs Banks, so they are not using that one. They must have got another from somewhere. A rental?'

Matthews just nodded his head, and said, 'Good work, keep me updated, thank you.'

Monteith and Watson stood looking at each other wondering what had just happened. Matthews rarely spoke to them directly unless he had to, never mind compliment them.

CHAPTER THIRTY-THREE

TUESDAY

One of the things detectives hate is early morning call-outs. Another is early morning calls when it's raining, and this morning at 6 a.m. it was raining hard. A call had come in from an insomniac dog walker, who had been along the river near the weir at 5 a.m. and had spotted something tangled in the undergrowth overhanging the river.

Watson and Monteith stood on the riverside in their waterproof macs and wellingtons, under the bright lights of the arc lamps, looking like two drowned rats. Neither wanted to be there.

Across the river, about half a mile down from the weir, specialist police divers from the underwater search unit had released what was left of a human body from the undergrowth and weeds. With the rain the river level had risen, the weir was flowing fast, making the extraction difficult.

The divers hauled the body into their boat and brought it over to the other bank. Twenty minutes later, the bloated body was on the grassy river bank, laid out on a sheet of plastic. Its macabre state was enough to turn the stomach of the best rescue workers, but Mac was in his element giving it the once-over before taking the body back to the morgue.

Mac's assistant was busy taking photographs of the body, recording the state they had found it in. It still had its running shirt, shorts and trainers on. Because of the bloating they were very tight and close to splitting.

Watson stood close by, but Monteith had had enough. One sight of the body and he had retreated to a safe distance.

'I can't do a lot at the moment with the body because of the bloating,' Mac said to Watson. 'I have to wait until the air and methane gas come out before I can start on the process. What I can tell you with some certainty is our body is male, that's it.'

'So you can't tell us how he died or when?'

'No, as I said, not until I get him on the slab later. Bodies in water react differently during decomposition which makes timelines difficult to work out.' Mac turned to his assistants once he had finished. 'You can bag him up.'

'Sorry, I cannot be more helpful at the moment.'

Mac walked back towards the weir with Watson and Monteith. Further down the river, the underwater search unit were checking over their equipment.

'Don't worry Mac, looks like an accident anyway,' Monteith talked as if it was not worth their time. 'He probably slipped in, got caught by the current and drowned.'

'Thank you Dr Monteith,' Mac said sarcastically. 'Maybe you can do the post-mortem with me? I value your expert opinion.' Mac looked at Watson who was trying not to laugh.

'No bleeding way. I'll leave that to you.' Monteith shook his head, as Mac and Watson burst out laughing.

Watson looked around the surrounding area as they approached the weir. 'If he didn't go in where we found the body, where did he fall in?'

'Judging from the flow of the river, anywhere from the weir downwards? But that's for you to work out. I only deal with the bodies,' Mac replied.

-X-

Crompton was waiting for them when they got into the office later that morning. He was speaking animatedly to Lorimer, who was updating the board with photographs and details.

'It's nice of you to join us! Did you have a good early morning walk by the river?' Crompton joked.

'Oh, it was lovely Boss, you should have joined us. Walking in the rain with the ones you love,' Watson said while staring longingly at Monteith.

'Well, Terry, you say the nicest things.' Monteith acted like a lovestruck teenager and batted his eyes back at Watson while giving him a peck on the cheek, together skipping hand-in-hand over to the information board.

'So the Secret Policeman's Ball is alive and well then.' Crompton was trying not to laugh. 'Listen, we have some new information. I would like to introduce you to Andrew McNulty and Thomas Smith.' He pointed to the new images on the board.

'These two lovely people killed Littlewood's wife, and are due to be released from HMP Claythorn this Friday. Now we need to be there before Littlewood and take them into protective custody until we catch Littlewood. I can't stress enough that we need to get this right. I don't want this bastard killing anyone else, let alone these two. He's been one step ahead of us but now we can stop him. I have spoken to the governor of Claythorn prison and arranged for McNulty and Smith to be handed over to us before they leave. I want all three of you to take an unmarked Range Rover and pick them up as soon as they're released and bring them back here.'

'Have we any idea where Littlewood and his daughter are now?' Watson said.

'No, looks like he has gone to ground somewhere. After ditching his car and leaving his daughter's at home, we don't know what they're driving now. All rental places we have talked to don't recognise him and have no record of a Littlewood renting a car.'

'All forces are on the look-out for him so if he's spotted we'll know about it.' Crompton's phone rang, 'Excuse me.'

'So when are you two moving in together?' Lorimer said mischievously.

'When our divorces come through, sweetheart, sorry.' Watson replied.

Monteith went to kiss him but Lorimer moved quickly away. 'Sorry you're not my type.'

Crompton reappeared from his office. 'Right, Lorimer. Can you organise that Range Rover with the car pool for Friday. You two, Matthews wants to see us now in his office.'

'In his office? What for?' Watson said. Crompton's withering look told him. 'Oh right,' he mumbled.

After taking the lift up to the fourth floor, they walked along the corridor and into Matthews's outer office. His PA, Beryl, stared at them over her glasses with a face that looked like she was sucking a lemon. 'Go straight in, he's expecting you.'

Being called to the super's office was akin to being called to the headmaster's office at school. You were either there to accept an award, or for disciplinary reasons. Normally only section heads entered for high-powered meetings.

Matthews was sitting behind his large desk typing on his computer. To his left was a bookcase which stretched the length of the wall. It contained not only books but also files and personal items. In front of the desk were three leather-backed wooden chairs.

'Be seated, I won't be a minute.' Matthews finished typing, and clicked a few things with the mouse.

'Right gentlemen, following your little escapade to the casino the other night, yes, DS Watson and DS Monteith, I have seen the CCTV clip, I have managed to put out the fire.'

Monteith tried to speak but Matthews stopped him. 'Don't thank me now because there will be repercussions. I have spoken to the editor of the newspaper and they will not run the story, either online or in the paper. DS Watson, now I know the full facts and you were only there because you wanted to keep an eye on your partner and nothing else, you don't need to stay and you can go back downstairs.'

'I would like to stay if you don't mind, Sir. Yes, he is my partner but he is also a good friend.' Watson stood firm looking at Monteith as if to say, 'I've got your back.'

'Very well, as long as you are okay with it?' Matthews looked at Monteith, who nodded affirmatively.

'As for you, DS Monteith, I am putting a record of this on your file. Jimmy Russell, as we all know, is one of the biggest crooks around here. But we have never had a chance to get a sniff of him never mind get close to him. Until now.'

Monteith was starting to feel uncomfortable. Why was Matthews talking about Russell in the way he was?

'We want you to get close to him. You've already seen inside his casino, spoken to him, shared a table with him, so you're the best person we know who could do this.'

Monteith shook his head, not wanting to believe what Matthews was suggesting. 'You mean you don't want a scandal, that's why you silenced the newspaper. You're nuts, you're putting a target on my back and hanging me out to dry.'

Matthews continued as if he hadn't heard Monteith's outburst, 'We will also pay off your five thousand pound gambling debt, and may give you some extra cash to help with your assignment. You can use it how you wish, but you need to report back to us what you have spent and what on. And let me be clear, if you get into trouble again with your gambling you're on your own. We will not bail you out a second time.'

CHAPTER THIRTY-FOUR

TUESDAY EVENING

Monteith sat in his car, his stomach turning somersaults. Each half of his brain felt like it was against the other in a WWE wrestling match: one fall, submission or a knockout. On the seat next to him was an envelope containing the five grand Matthews had given him to pay off Russell. Five grand which did not just come with strings attached, but came with a hangman's noose. He didn't want to know whether Matthews or Russell was going to pull the lever on the trap door. Both had become judge, jury and executioner on his job and ultimately his life.

He had phoned ahead prior to leaving the station, making sure Jimmy Russell would be in. Now here he was, sat in front of the casino contemplating his next move.

The casino was almost empty with it being early evening as Monteith entered. The main trade, the high rollers, came in later and spent enough to keep a small country out of debt. Standing just inside the doors were the same two bouncers who'd escorted him in on his last visit. They already knew why he was there.

As they came out of the lift, Jimmy Russell was deep in conversation with his brother Allan, looking at a

159

large sheet of paper and pointing as they looked over the balcony at the casino floor below.

'Mr Monteith, please join us.' Jimmy Russell beckoned him over. As Monteith stood by him, Jimmy put an arm around his shoulder.

'We were discussing making some changes. Adding some more things in, more fruit machines, another blackjack table. We are also thinking of adding a men-only club in one of the rooms at the back. Maximising revenue streams, what do you think?'

'Erm, I don't know. If you think you need to then go ahead,' Monteith garbled.

'See Allan, even Mr Monteith here thinks it's a good idea,' Russell said, slapping him on the back. 'But discussing this is not why you're here.' Russell's demeanour changed instantly.

Monteith dug around in his jacket, pulling out the envelope of money. 'It's all there, your five grand.'

Russell took the envelope and opened it, smiling. He nodded to the bouncers who grabbed Monteith by the arms, holding him. Monteith struggled but it was in vain.

'Thank you, Mr Monteith, now that was not hard to do.' Russell patted him on the cheek, demeaning him. 'See Mr Monteith back to his car, lads. Oh this time, be careful.' Russell pocketed the envelope and both Russell brothers walked off to their inner sanctum.

CHAPTER THIRTY-FIVE

WEDNESDAY MORNING

The mortuary had almost become a second home to Watson and Monteith over the last few weeks. Now they were there for the autopsy of the man who'd been brought out of the river the previous morning.

Mac and his assistant were dressed in all their finery: green scrubs, yellow wellies and gloves, and masks which looked like they came from the local welders.

Both the detectives, standing away from the table, were kitted out in the same gear except for the gloves and their masks were made from paper.

It was all too much for Monteith, who emptied the contents of his breakfast into a nearby sink before staggering out of the door, his face the colour of his scrubs, even before Mac had begun.

After cutting away the victim's clothes and giving it a clean, Mac came across something of interest. He removed his mask. 'Terry, I think I've found how he died.'

Mac's assistant started taking photos of where he was pointing. Watson approached the table, his hand holding his mask closer to his face, trying to avoid the stench of the corpse.

Mac pointed to two holes in the body's chest. 'It

looks like he was shot before he ended up in the river. I will see if the bullets are still in there when I open him up.'

'I take it there was no ID on him?'

'No, I will have to use his teeth for ID. His fingertips have been eaten by fish, along with other parts of his body.'

Mac showed Watson the damaged fingers, ears and lips. The victim moaned as trapped gases escaped his mouth. Watson backed away from the table as the stench grew stronger.

'Jesus, that's rank. How can you work on a body like this?'

'We don't get many bloaters, but you get used to it after a while. The fire victims are the worst. It takes forever to get the smell of smoke and burnt flesh out of here. The sales of air fresheners go up when we have one of those,' Mac said.

'I will check the missing persons reports when I get back, somebody has to be wondering where he is. Thanks Mac.' Watson started towards the door. He could feel the contents of his own stomach groaning for release.

'Don't you want to stay for the examination?' Mac said, holding up his scalpel. 'I was just about to cut him open.'

'Can I quote you? You do the bodies; the rest is for us to work out.'

-X-

Littlewood and Susan were relaxing at their woodland retreat.

They sunbathed on the decking, walked along the miles of woodland trails, and even did a spot of swimming in the camp's indoor pool.

While there, Susan noticed she was being eyed up

by some of the younger men who were trying to outdo each other, posing around the sides of the pool. Flattered by all the attention she wished it was at a different time and place. Littlewood had also noticed from where he was sitting. He smiled with pride, his daughter being the centre of attention for once.

She'd had a crap upbringing. He knew that. Helping a depressive alcoholic after her mother's murder was something no child should have to go through. But she had, and she had now bloomed into a beautiful young woman.

'Why don't you go and enjoy yourself?' Littlewood suggested to Susan, as she came back to the table.

'No. I came with you. We are on holiday together.'

'Listen, I will be all right. Tomorrow we have a big day ahead of us. You need to let your hair down. You've been looking after me for years. It's time you did something for yourself.'

'But Dad!'

'No, buts.' Littlewood put a hand on her arm and spoke softly. 'I've seen those men over there looking at you. Go and talk to them, enjoy yourself. I will be fine.'

Susan smiled. 'Thanks Dad.'

-X-

When Watson and Monteith arrived back at the station, Monteith ran directly into the toilets. Seeing the latest body at the morgue had really affected him. Watson had to drive Monteith's car back, stopping on the way because Monteith needed to throw up again.

'Where's Keith?' Lorimer said, as Watson walked into the office.

He was at his computer with Crompton looking through the latest missing persons list. Watson had phoned through with an update when he stopped for

Monteith on the way back.

'Kermit's in the toilet groaning down the big white telephone. That last body really turned his stomach.'

'Kermit?' Lorimer laughed out loud. 'It was that bad?'

'Oh, yes. Even I struggled, but survived,' Watson laughed.

'I had better see how he is.' Crompton sighed, as he headed for the toilets.

'How are you doing with missing persons?' Watson said to Lorimer, as he made himself a drink.

'We have only just started. There's a few out there, but none at the moment match our body. We might have to wait until Mac has done his business.'

Monteith was washing his face when Crompton entered. 'How are you, Keith?'

Monteith stood up and grabbed a handful of paper towels. 'I'll be fine boss. Just give me ten minutes.'

'Did you pay Russell off last night?' Crompton enquired.

'Yes. He was discussing something with his brother when I got there. I couldn't stay. As soon as I paid him his goons threw me out.'

'Did you catch what they were discussing?'

'Catch it? He told me! They are going to expand the casino. Bringing in a men-only club.' Monteith's face was quickly tuning from green to a lovely chalk-white colour.

'Interesting.'

CHAPTER THIRTY-SIX

EARLY THURSDAY MORNING

Littlewood and Susan packed up their things and started their journey back into West Ravenswood. Dawn was breaking and the sun shone brightly, lighting their way to their final destination. The beauty of renting a 4x4 instead of using either of their cars was to reduce the risk of being seen, and hopefully slip back into the city unnoticed. Keeping off the main roads added to their safety.

Nothing was said once they set off. That had been done back in the cabin, father to daughter, daughter to father. Between them, a plan had been worked out, and how it was to be carried out.

It was a bit like entering the lion's den. Would the police be there? Would they be able to get McNulty and Smith without raising suspicion? Would they bump into someone from Claythorn who recognised them?

They had come this far, none of that would now put them off.

Littlewood pulled into the visitors' car park, parking close enough to the prison that if everything went to plan they could be in and out quickly. Littlewood looked at Susan and smiled. 'Thank you for everything.' A tear rolled down his cheek.

'We are family and family comes first.' Susan got out and waited on the path, away from everyone else waiting for their loved ones.

The pickup went easier than they thought it would go. Smith and McNulty came like lambs to the slaughter. Well, they weren't given a chance of doing anything else. Susan stuck her father's gun in the ribs of McNulty, telling them if they did anything stupid she would kill them on the spot.

Susan glanced around before instructing Smith and McNulty to walk in front of her to the 4x4. The gun still close to McNulty's ribs. Littlewood had already opened the back door ready for their guests.

When they got into the 4x4, Smith and McNulty's hands were bound with Ty-Raps. They were told not to make any sudden moves alerting anyone or they would be shot on the spot.

Littlewood drove out of the car park, trying not to attract attention from the other just-released prisoners and their families. Susan was in the back, making sure their guests behaved.

Littlewood headed for wasteland close to the disused industrial buildings on the edge of the city. A brownfield area down for redevelopment but nothing had started yet due to council planning dragging their heels.

He pulled into one of the derelict warehouses and parked up. McNulty and Smith, unsurprisingly, had become agitated on the drive over, but thankfully for all of them they tried nothing in the way of causing trouble.

Littlewood jumped out, opened the rear door and pulled a screaming McNulty out, dragging him around the back of the 4x4. Susan, brandishing the gun, ordered Smith out the other side, forcing them to kneel next to each other in the dirt and rubbish on the ground.

Littlewood paced slowly in front of McNulty and

Smith. 'Let me introduce myself. My name is Colin Littlewood, and you murdered my wife and Susan's mother.'

'But we didn't,' McNulty stuttered.

'Shut up,' Littlewood roared. 'I don't want to hear your snivelling or pity. It won't help where you are going.'

'She fell, we didn't touch her,' Smith shouted.

Susan pointed the gun at him. 'Did you not hear my father? Shut up.'

'You were still in our house, you were robbing us. If you had not been in our house, she would not have died. You killed my wife.' Littlewood's face was just inches away from Smith's, looking straight into the frightened man's eyes.

Smith turned his face away, eyes shut tight. Littlewood raged and punched him twice in the face. Smith howled in pain, his nose dripping blood.

McNulty didn't miss out, as Littlewood kicked him in the stomach, making him keel over sideways, coughing and gasping for air. Littlewood dragged him back up to a kneeling position and unloaded a couple of punches to his face.

Susan, standing by their 4x4, looked at her father, at the hatred in his eyes. She understood the anger he was feeling, and knew it had to be released. He had waited ten years for this moment. Alcohol hadn't released it, neither had killing Freeman, Davis or Knowles.

'You're a nutter, a lunatic. You're the one that should be locked up,' Smith shouted. For that outburst he got a kick in the stomach, followed by a flurry of punches to the face. Smith tried to cover his face but with his hands tied couldn't protect himself.

Littlewood grabbed him by the hair and pulled him back up.

Susan was getting worried. She had never seen her father like this before. 'Dad!'

He looked at her with glazed-over eyes and puffed hard, trying to get has breath back.

'Dad, can we finish this?' She handed over the gun. 'Let's get out of here.'

Littlewood looked down at the weapon and then at McNulty and Smith. Both were staring back at him, shouting at him, but he could not hear them. He was in a world of his own. He stepped forward and pressed the end of the barrel against McNulty's forehead. McNulty was screaming. Littlewood pulled the gun away and pressed it against Smith's forehead, causing Smith to try to pull away. Littlewood hit him on the head with the gun for that. Blood started rolling down from the gash it made.

'Dad, shoot them!' Susan didn't like what she was seeing. When working this out they had decided to just shoot them and disappear. Her father's actions was scaring her. Littlewood looked at Susan with a wicked smile on his face.

'No Susan, we aren't going to kill them here. Shooting's too good for them. I have a better idea.'

'What are you talking about? We had it all sorted.' Susan began hyperventilating.

Littlewood laughed. 'Get them back into the 4x4, we are going for a little drive.'

'Where? Tell me, Dad? I'm getting worried.'

Littlewood walked across to Susan, resting his hand on her cheek. 'The multi-storey. Chucking them off the top of there seems a fitting end for them, considering.'

'But Dad?'

Littlewood shot her a venomous look. 'Are you not behind me anymore?'

'Yes, of course I am. It's just that we had a plan and

now you want to change it.'

'Right, get them in the car and you're driving.' He threw the keys at her, signalling the end of the discussion.

They bungled McNulty and Smith into the back of the 4x4, making them lie on the floor so no one could see them. Littlewood put masking tape over their mouths, mainly to stop them whining. A couple more swift punches to each of them added to the 'Do not move or else' threat.

Susan pulled out of the warehouse and started driving back into the city. Littlewood was in the passenger seat, gun on his lap. She didn't know what to make of her father. He had done a complete U-turn in the way he was behaving. She had seen documentaries on serial killers and murderers. Some who acted as though what they had done was the norm. Just like her father, she realised with a gasp of shock.

She looked across at him. He was calm, as if out for a Sunday drive. There were few signs he could blow at any time. The manic look in his eyes. his legs twitching, glancing over his shoulder at their captives, fingering the trigger on the gun, stroking it like a pet.

Then it all went off.

They pulled up to a set of traffic lights. Beside them a police car drew up. One officer looked across and nudged his partner, who also looked and nodded. Littlewood smiled at the officers and wound down his window. Before they could react, Littlewood had fired at the car, taking out their windscreen.

'Drive!' he said to Susan, who, shaking with fear, slammed the car into gear and floored it.

Wheels screeching, the 4x4 launched forward into traffic. Susan managed not to hit anything as they took off down the road.

'What the hell did you do that for?' Susan yelled.

'They had recognised us.'

'But you did not have to shoot at them for Christ's sake.' Susan was looking in her rear-view mirror, checking they were not being followed.

'Shut up and get us to the multi-storey.'

CHAPTER THIRTY-SEVEN

'Hey Karl, when do you take your detective's exam? It must be soon,' Watson said, as he walked past Lorimer's desk, heading for a coffee refill.

'In a month's time,' Lorimer said, leaning back in his chair. 'I was up till one this morning revising.'

'We'll make a detective of you yet,' Monteith swung round on his chair, joining in.

'If you need help, you only need to ask,' Watson said.

'Cheers lads, it's been . . .' Lorimer paused, choosing his words carefully, 'entertaining, seeing how you work.'

Monteith laughed. Getting up, he joined Watson at Lorimer's desk. 'So we haven't put you off detective work?'

'No, on the contrary, helping you has made me more determined to pass the exam.'

'That's good to hear,' Watson said, 'because I have heard that the bosses have agreed to the extension of this agency, and are interviewing newly trained Detective Constables.'

The banter and chat was ended quickly as all three turned to see Crompton slamming both his fists hard onto his desk.

'I wonder who's upset the boss,' Monteith mused as he released a surge of expletives.

Watson nodded towards Crompton's office. 'It looks like we're about to find out.'

Crompton stormed out of his office, its door nearly coming off its hinges as he grabbed it.

'They were released this morning,' Crompton shouted across the room. His face red with rage. 'They fucking released McNulty and Smith this morning!'

'What do you mean they were released this morning? We were told it would be tomorrow.' Monteith nearly spilled his coffee.

'I've just got off the phone with the governor. He told me that McNulty and Smith were released at 8 a.m.'

Watson looked at his watch. It was 9.30 a.m. 'They could be anywhere by now,' Watson said, frustrated. 'Who picked them up? Their families?'

'I don't have a clue. The governor didn't know. He was in a meeting. It seems once they are out of their front gates, they're not the prison's problem.' Crompton was fuming. 'I've told him we want to see CCTV coverage of their front gate as soon as possible. If not, I will charge him with obstruction.' Crompton grabbed his coat, sending the coat stand flying. 'I'm going there straight away. Watson, Monteith you are coming with me. At least you can stop me from hitting him.'

Twenty minutes later, Crompton's anger hadn't subsided. Nothing Monteith and Watson said during the drive over calmed the situation.

As soon as Monteith parked up in the visitors' car park, Crompton jumped out and stormed up the path leading to the main door. Watson was half out of the car calling after him, 'Boss, wait. Sir?'

He caught up to Crompton as he opened the door into the reception. 'Hang on.'

Crompton let go of the door. 'What?'

'They won't let you see anyone if you go in there like Storming Norman. This is not your territory, and you cannot go in there and throw your weight around.'

Crompton pointed towards the door. 'But they have just possibly released two men into the arms of a wanted killer. What the hell were they doing?'

'Their job,' Watson said.

Monteith joined them as they continued arguing. 'Just to let you know, we are being watched.' Looking up they saw the CCTV camera above them. 'They have trained it on you two since you started.'

Watson took control. 'When we go in, just stand back and compose yourself. I will book us in.' Approaching the reception desk he introduced himself to one of the security officers behind the plexiglass. 'DCI Crompton, DS Watson and DS Monteith to see Governor Greenslade. We are expected.' All three of them showed the receptionist their IDs.

They were escorted upstairs and into a side office and asked to wait. The office was fitted out with CCTV monitors and recording equipment. Two officers sat in front of the bank of equipment. The screens showed every part of the prison.

'Where is he?' Crompton mumbled under his breath, watching the daily routine and ritual of prison life.

'Be patient.' Watson knew his boss was still on a short fuse.

The door opened and in strode Governor Greenslade, a blue manila-coloured folder in his hand. He looked like a headmaster of old. Greying hair, rounded metal glasses, shirt, tie, jumper and checked jacket.

'Sorry to keep you waiting gentlemen, my PA suddenly rang in saying she was taking a few days off and I have had trouble finding the relevant paperwork. I have had to rearrange an important meeting because of this.

Have we got the CCTV footage from this morning?' he asked one of the officers.

'Yes, Sir. It's all set up.'

'Who was it you were interested in, Detective Chief Inspector?' Greenslade acted as if he could not be bothered with it all.

'Mr Greenslade,' Crompton said through gritted teeth. 'I am sorry we have ruined your morning, but we believe two of your former guests are in danger. And we would like to find out why they were released twenty-four hours before the date we were told, and who picked them up. Now if it's not too much trouble, we would like to see the footage. And I hope you have a very good explanation for what the hell went on.' By the time he had stopped berating the governor, his voice had gone up three octaves and he was so close to Greenslade, he could count the hairs up his nose.

'Can we see the pictures Craig?' Greenslade said to one of the officers sitting watching the CCTV footage.

The first clip was of fourteen men milling inside the reception area, ready to be released. Some stood talking to each other. Others paced around, eager to get out and into the arms of their loved ones. Some stood on their own, probably contemplating what was on the other side of the main gate. Life questions which because of having been incarcerated for years, they hadn't needed to think about until now.

'Which ones are McNulty and Smith?' Monteith said to Craig.

'They're the two in the back corner,' Craig pointed them out. They were not talking to anyone, keeping themselves to themselves.

'Do inmates get released every day?' Monteith was intrigued.

'Yes, except for weekends and bank holidays. If their release date falls on one of those days they go on a

Friday.'

'Is there a limit to the number you release at the same time?'

'No, if it's your time you go. You could be the only one that day, or you could be one of many like these.' He emphasized his point by tapping on the top of the screen.

Monteith looked closer at the prisoners being released now. 'Hey Terry, have a look at this. Isn't that Justin Taylor?'

Watson joined him and looked at the man that Monteith was pointing to.

'Yes, my God! Didn't we put him away for those jewellery raids five years ago? And look, there's Darren Barnes. He was done for glassing that bloke in the Carpenters Arms.'

'I remember,' Monteith said. 'GBH wasn't it? The bloke lost an eye in the attack.'

'When you two have stopped playing guess the crime . . . It looks like they are on their way out, now concentrate,' Crompton said, still on Gas Mark four: simmering but close to the boil.

The inmates were walking out of the reception area and out towards the large metal front gate. The time on the tape read 8 a.m. McNulty and Smith were still keeping their distance from the other men. The CCTV footage switched over to view beyond the gate. Relatives were gathered waiting for their loved ones. A line of taxis were parked close by if needed or had already been booked. Some disappeared for the walk into town to catch the next bus or train out of the city, wanting to get as far away from Claythorn as they could.

McNulty and Smith had just come out. They were in the bottom left hand side of the screen. They watched them exit the gate and walk towards the city centre. As they got close to the visitors' car park, a woman moved from where she had been standing, approaching them.

She looked like she knew them and started talking.

'Who is she? Does anybody know?' Crompton said, getting wound up again.

'That's Susan Farmer, my PA,' Greenslade said, his voice shaking.

They all turned to look at him.

Greenslade looked confused. 'She rang in to say that she was taking a few days off. She was going away with her father because he was not well.'

'Well, it doesn't look like she's gone anywhere to me,' Crompton snapped back. 'How does she know McNulty and Smith?'

'I don't know, honestly.'

'Look at this!' Watson said. Susan was now escorting McNulty and Smith through the visitor's car park. 'She's got them at bloody gunpoint.'

They watched as the woman, now identified as Susan Farmer, made Smith and McNulty get into the back of a 4x4, a gun in her hand. A man in the driver's seat turned to speak to McNulty and Smith.

'Is there another camera in the visitors' car park, so we can see what went on?'

'I will check,' Craig pushed a few buttons searching for the relevant piece of archived footage.

Crompton chose that time to let rip at the governor. 'Mr Greenslade, how the hell were they released twenty-four hours before they should have been? Any ideas, because I'm damned if I'm leaving this here, especially after what I have just seen.'

CHAPTER THIRTY-EIGHT

'I have CCTV from the visitors' car park,' Craig shouted above the commotion. Monteith and Watson stood looking over Craig's shoulders at the screens.

'I've not finished,' Crompton warned Greenslade.

The first couple of minutes showed what they had already seen, albeit from a different angle, so the operator fast-forwarded the footage to when Susan had stuck the gun into the side of McNulty making sure they knew she was not messing around, and they headed off into the car park.

'Didn't anyone see this happen at the time?' Monteith said.

Both the officers operating the equipment shook their heads.

Back on the screen, Susan, McNulty and Smith had reached the 4x4. The driver of the vehicle visible.

'That's Littlewood!' Watson exclaimed. 'Shit, they have McNulty and Smith.'

'That must be his daughter,' Monteith said, not wanting to believe what he was seeing.

They watched as McNulty and Smith were shoved into the back of the 4x4. Words were exchanged, mainly from Littlewood and his daughter and it looked like the gun was waved in their faces as a warning. Littlewood then drove the 4x4 out of the car park in the direction of the city centre.

Monteith and Watson stood looking at each other. Crompton broke the silence with exactly what they was thinking.

'Well, that was one big fuck up we have just seen. And Greenslade, I am looking at the biggest fuck up here. This is your entire fault. You released two inmates into the hands of the two people who want them dead. I want to see your paperwork. If anything happens to them I am holding you responsible.'

Greenslade handed him the folder he was holding. 'All the details are in there.'

Watson's phone rang, he went out of the room to take it.

Crompton opened the file Greenslade had given him and started reading. 'According to this official printout from your records, McNulty and Smith were to have been released tomorrow. But the copy of the release letters which were given to them give a release date of today.'

Crompton waved them at Greenslade. 'Who writes out these letters?'

'Susan, my PA, once I have seen and confirmed the details of the Parole Board.'

'Your PA, who we have just seen take Andrew McNulty and Thomas Smith at gun point away from the prison. And you don't check these letters before they are given to your inmates?'

'No, I'd no need to. I trusted Susan.'

Before Crompton could lose his temper again with Greenslade, Watson came flying back into the room.

'That was the control room. Littlewood's 4x4 was spotted by uniform, but Littlewood shot at their car as he took off, taking out their windscreen. Another squad car saw Littlewood enter the multi-storey in the city centre. They believe he has driven up to the top level. Uniform have shut off the entire car park and have called armed response.'

Crompton was enraged by the time it took them to get out of the prison, with having to get through all the security. He sat in the back of Monteith's BMW cursing.

They received a police squad car escort to get them through the traffic for the final mile. The roads around the multi-storey had been closed off. The police had this down to a tee seeing as the multi-storey was a favourite place for the desperate and the despondent to end their lives by jumping off it.

Monteith pulled up by the entrance, where Lorimer was talking to several of the emergency services helping with their co-ordination. Lorimer jogged across and jumped in the back of their car.

'What's happening?' Crompton said, still stressed out.

'Littlewood's 4x4 was spotted about twenty minutes ago by a vigilant PC at a set of traffic lights. Shots were fired at the squad car by someone in Littlewood's vehicle, shattering the windscreen. Neither officer were hit. Another car took up the pursuit. No attempt was taken to stop the 4x4, and they followed him at a safe distance to this car park, up onto the top level. Littlewood is parked at one end, and the squad car is at the other. They have not approached Littlewood and as far as I am aware no one has got out of his 4x4. We have cleared the car park up to the level below. The cars on the top are still there, the owners are being kept together away from the area, but close enough to fetch them when it's safe. The firearms unit has arrived and is on the level below, along with the hostage negotiator.' Lorimer's run down was thorough. They could hear the police helicopter flying above them.

'Keith let's get up there and see what's happening.' Monteith swung the car around and headed through the police cordon at the entrance of the multi-storey.

Driving up the ramps onto the deserted levels was eerie. Nobody in Monteith's car said anything, they were all looking at the vacant spaces in the concrete monolith.

Monteith inched his car up onto the sixth level, Watson showing his ID to the officers already there. They parked up and walked over, meeting up with the head of the Armed Response Unit, putting on the flak jackets they were handed.

The armed officer then updated them. 'The suspect's car has been static for about fifteen minutes. There are four people in the car. Two in the front and two in the back. There isn't much movement coming from the back, but the two in the front have been in animated conversation.'

Crompton nodded. 'Can we get up on the next level?'

'Yes, I can take you up there but we need to be cautious. We don't know what this Littlewood fella is likely to do. Your sergeant here filled us in on what happened earlier on. I don't want to take any chances. If I tell you to move back down here, you do it. Are you ready?'

'When you are,' Crompton said.

Just as they started up the ramp, there was a cracking voice over the officer's radio. 'Movement at the car, doors being opened.'

The armed officer listened. 'Anybody getting out?'

'Two in front out. Opening back doors, two people in back being dragged out of car. Looks like they are tied up.'

'Let's move up. But remember, trouble and . . .'

Crompton nodded his assent.

The armed officer slowly went up the last ramp

onto the top level. They spaced out using the cars which had been trapped up there as cover. Crompton, Watson, Monteith and Lorimer came up behind and were told to stay back until things were clearer.

CHAPTER THIRTY-NINE

Littlewood and Susan were out of the 4x4, standing by the outside wall. In-between them, on the ground, were McNulty and Smith. Below, the road leading to the car park was deserted of traffic. Police cars and tape blocked the way. The only vehicles visible were emergency vehicles waiting in case they were needed.

Watson took a chance. Crouching down, he ran to get a better view from a nearby car that was parked closer to the action, but still behind the armed officers.

'Where the hell are you going?' Monteith was surprised at Watson's movement.

'I need to see what's going on.' Watson was on his knees behind the car, quickly signalling for Monteith to join him. Watson stuck his head up, looking over the car's bonnet.

'What can you see?' Monteith said.

'Littlewood and Susan are standing by the 4x4.'

'Any sign of McNulty and Smith?'

Waston struggled to see, 'No, I can only see . . . no wait, I see them. They're next to Littlewood on the ground. It looks like Littlewood's beaten them up. They have tape over their mouths and it looks like they've got their hands tied.

Crompton and Lorimer had moved closer as well, behind another car on the other side of the level.

At the other end, the Littlewoods were arguing so much they didn't seem to notice the armed responders.

'Dad, this is not what we agreed.'

'Yes, well I told you I had a better idea for these scumbags.' Littlewood kicked McNulty again, just for the hell of it.

'Dad, please think about–'

'I've had ten years of thinking. About your mother, and the life we could have been living if it wasn't for these two bastards. Ten years thinking of the things I could do to them. Ten years thinking about this day. Ten wasted years.' Littlewood grabbed Thomas Smith and dragged him up, giving him another punch in the stomach.

'Colin Littlewood, Susan. This is the West Ravenswood police. Please put down your weapons and release your hostages,' the voice of the negotiator boomed out through a loudhailer, stopping Littlewood in his tracks.

Both looked around at the officers, who had their firearms trained on them.

'Colin, what can we do to end this peacefully?' the negotiator said.

'Justice, for my wife,' Littlewood shouted. 'For these two miserable cowards, to pay for what they did.'

Crompton had had enough. He moved out from behind the car and tried to grab the loudhailer from the negotiators hands but was thankful prevented from doing so by a rational hand on his shoulder.

'Put your weapons down,' the negotiator said.

'No, I'm not,' Littlewood roared, pushing Smith closer to the edge of the multi-storey. Grabbing Smith's collar and belt, lifting, and pushing him over the ledge, causing him to scream in fear.

'Dad, no!' Susan blurted out. 'I am not being a part of this. We had an agreement. I have had enough.'

Susan turned and ran towards the police, 'Don't shoot. I'm giving myself up.'

'Stop right there,' one of the armed officers ordered. Susan stopped straight away, standing there with tears streaming down her face.

'Down on the floor and hands on your head.' Susan did as she was told and got down on her knees, lying face-down on the cold concrete.

Four armed officers moved forward to surround her, cuffing her then lifting her to walk her to safety right before a burst of gunfire caught everybody off-guard.

'Who fired?' The head of the ARU was shouting. 'I gave no order to fire.'

Everyone looked around, wondering who it had been.

'Boss? What the hell are you doing?' Watson was staring at Crompton. He was standing with the negotiators gun pulled at arm's length. One of the armed responders on the floor beside him just regaining his footing.

'Terry, look!' Monteith was pointing.

Colin Littlewood was lying on the floor. McNulty and Smith were crouched flat against the far wall.

A small group of armed officers made their way over to Littlewood slowly, covering each other. One checked Littlewood, feeling for a pulse. Three gunshot wounds were visible: one in his head and two in his torso. The armed officer confirmed over the radio that Littlewood was dead.

'Boss, give me the gun,' Watson spoke slowly to Crompton, 'please.'

Crompton turned his head towards Watson. His eyes were glazed over.

'He wanted justice. I have just given it to him,'

Crompton said in a harsh tone. 'And justice for Elizabeth Preston.'

Watson remained calm. 'Boss, the gun, and please don't say anything else.'

Crompton nodded, letting Watson take the gun. He handed the firearm over to an ARU officer, who placed it into a clear evidence bag and tagged it.

'Detective Chief Inspector Crompton, I am arresting you for the murder of Colin Littlewood. You do not have to say anything. But it may harm your defence if you do not mention when questioned something which you later rely on in court. Anything you do say may be given in evidence.'

As soon as Watson had cautioned their superior Monteith cuffed and guided Crompton back to a waiting squad car.

Everyone was silently watching as the car set off down the ramp and out of the multi-storey towards the custody suite.

CHAPTER FORTY

Nobody felt like celebrating when they were back at headquarters. Yes, they had got a serial killer off the streets, but not in the way they had wanted.

DCI Crompton had been booked in. Watson, Monteith and Lorimer had the ignominy of seeing their boss having his name taken for the records, and why he was arrested. Having his mug shot and fingerprints taken. Having to watch as his personal items, belt, shoelaces and uniform were taken from him and bagged up. Seeing him being escorted down to the cells, dressed in a paper boiler suit, the door banged shut behind him.

The next few days were taken up with paperwork, lots of it. The Independent Office of Police Complaints had been brought in to oversee everything. They interviewed Watson, Monteith and Lorimer separately regarding the killing of Colin Littlewood.

They had transferred Crompton to a police station out of West Ravenswood for his interviews. Though conducting them had been a waste of time as the only thing Crompton had said was, 'No comment.'

Susan Littlewood was released from hospital into police custody. She was arrested and interviewed over her part in the kidnappings and murders. She said her father made her do everything. She was frightened of him and went along with what he wanted. From getting the job at the prison to helping compile the list in the red book, which the forensic technicians found while searching the Littlewoods' home. Now she was on her own.

Littlewood's red book contained a list of seventeen names, four of which had been crossed out. Ronald Freeman, Jackson Davis, Adrian Knowles, and Duncan Healey. Healey's name was passed on to Mac as a possible name for the bloated body found in the river.

As Watson and Monteith scanned the list, three names popped out, those of Billy, Davy and Joseph Clayton. How close had they been to becoming Littlewood's next victims?

The CDA needed a new leader. Watson and Monteith had been there the longest, but they knew Matthews would bring someone in from another area. Watson had been a stand-in until they installed the new boss. Rumours had been doing the rounds about who it could be.

Watson, Monteith and Lorimer were going through the cases they were working on, when a smiling Matthews walked into the office. With him was a smartly dressed lady in a black pant suit with a cream blouse, carrying a briefcase. She stood by him as he called the office to order.

'Ladies and gentlemen if I can have your attention. I would like to introduce you to the new boss of the CDA, DCI Tanya Wright.'

'Good afternoon detectives,' she said. 'It's good to finally meet you. I've heard a lot of good things about you all.'

Before they had a chance to reply, Matthews directed their new boss into DCI Crompton's old office and shut the door.

'Now that I was not expecting.' Monteith gestured towards the office.

'What, Matthews being kind or the new DCI?' Watson said.

'Both.'

Matthews came out of the office and walked straight past them without looking at them. DCI Wright stood in the office doorway.

'Hi all, if you would step this way please, I think it's time for some introductions.'

CHAPTER FORTY-ONE

ONE MONTH LATER

Monteith was glad his day had finished. Matthews had been pressing him again to get information on the Russell's, but he was getting nowhere with just being a patron of the casino. They kept their business and private lives separate. Trying to make a jerk like Matthews understand that was impossible.

Mac had confirmed the identity of the river body as Healey, adding another murder to Susan's charges of accessory to the fact.

Crompton was facing trial for the murder of Littlewood. He was being kept under close supervision in prison.

DCI Tanya Wright had come in and had hit the ground running. She was fair but tough when needed to be.

There was talk that as they didn't officially have one a Detective Inspector was needing promoting.

Watson had gone into town to meet his wife and children for a meal. Monteith, at least could relax for a couple of days before re-entering the madhouse that was the Criminal Detective Agency.

Walking towards his BMW Series 1, Monteith flicked through the text messages that had been left on his iPhone as he approached his car.

Two men dressed in dark clothing stepped out in front of him.

One of them smashed a right-handed punch into Monteith's face. The force of which sent him bouncing off the front wing of the car next to him. One of the men forced a hessian bag over his head and bound his hands behind his back with Ty-Raps before he had time to yell for help.

'What the hell? Who are you?' Monteith mumbled, feeling the full force of a kick to his stomach, which knocked the wind out of his lungs.

He heard a van pull up next to him and doors opening. Then he was hoisted off the ground and thrown into the back of the van. The doors slammed slut, the engine revved, then whoever was driving the van moved off.

'Got you,' Allan Russell said.

He sat in his car and watched the event unfolding from afar. He waited till the van had cleared the car park before he followed it at a safe distance.

Jimmy Russell was sampling one of the finest scotches in his collection, a Highland Park, distilled in 1974, and bottled in 2006. Only one hundred and forty-one bottles had ever been made.

A notification on his mobile phone disrupted him. It was a text message. He read it with a smile.

Your package has been collected.

ACKNOWLEDGEMENTS

I would like to thank Louise, Michael, and everyone else at Dark Edge Press for their hard work in publishing this book. They have made me feel very welcome, and I look forward to working with them.

I would also like to thank Ross Greenwood, for inviting me to the Dark Side of Fiction and for allowing me to bounce ideas off his head in relation to prison procedure for this book.

And Maureen Davis and Beryl Fielder, my beta readers.

To Kerrie Watson and Kerry Monteith. The original Watson & Monteith. It was a pleasure working with you.

And finally, I would like to thank you, my readers, for purchasing this book. I hope you have enjoyed it. Please leave a review with the vendor you purchased this title from. Reviews increase the visibility of books, helping other readers to find them.

Tony has worked as a lifeguard, both here and abroad, a white-van man, a baker, a civil servant for the MOD, and in Children and Adult Social Services for the local council. Ideas for a novel had been floating around in his head for some time before be put pen to paper and began writing his first novel.

Born in Warrington Cheshire in 1967 Tony moved to Rutland in 1981. He now lives in Peterborough with his wife, two nutty cats and a Romanian rescue dog. When not writing he likes to listen to Rock and Heavy Metal. Something he has in common with our Publishing Director.

Love crime fiction as much as we do?

Sign up to our associates program to be first in line to receive Advance Review Copies of our books, and to win stationary and signed, dedicated editions of our titles during our monthly competitions. Further details on our website: www.darkedgepress.co.uk

Follow @darkedgepress on Facebook, Twitter, and Instagram to stay updated on our latest releases.

Printed in Great Britain
by Amazon